Why couldn't he get Lisa Richardson out of his head?

This was the first time in three years that any woman had haunted his dreams. The first time in three years that he'd felt that pull of attraction. The first time in three years that he'd been aware of someone walking into a room even when his back was turned to the door.

But he couldn't let himself act on it. Couldn't take that risk again. It wasn't just his heart in danger: it was Lisa's too, when he turned out to be Mr Wrong and let her down.

He blitzed the house, hoping that the action of scrubbing things clean again would scrub all thoughts of Lisa from his head. He was *not* going to think about Lisa Richardson. Or speculate how soft her skin might be. Or wonder how it would feel to have that beautiful mouth tracking down his body…

BACHELOR DADS
Single Doctor…Single Father!

At work they are skilled medical professionals, but at home, as soon as they walk in the door, these eligible bachelors are on full-time fatherhood duty!

These devoted dads still find room in their lives for love…

It takes very special women to win the hearts of these dedicated doctors, and a very special kind of caring to make these single fathers full-time husbands!

THE CONSULTANT'S NEW-FOUND FAMILY

BY
KATE HARDY

MILLS & BOON™

Pure reading pleasure

First published in Great Britain 2007
Large Print edition 2007
Harlequin Mills & Boon Limited,
Eton House, 18-24 Paradise Road,
Richmond, Surrey TW9 1SR

© Pamela Brooks 2007

ISBN-13: 978 0 263 19368 8

Set in Times Roman 16½ on 18½ pt.
17-1007-49715

Printed and bound in Great Britain
by Antony Rowe Ltd, Chippenham, Wiltshire

Kate Hardy lives in Norwich, in the east of England, with her husband, two young children, one bouncy spaniel, and too many books to count! When she's not busy writing romance or researching local history, she helps out at her children's schools; she's a school governor and chair of the PTA. She also loves cooking—see if you can spot the recipes sneaked into her books! (They're also on her website, along with extracts and stories behind the books.)

Writing for Harlequin Mills & Boon has been a dream come true for Kate—something she wanted to do ever since she was twelve. She's been writing Medical Romance™ for nearly five years now, and also writes for the Modern Extra series. She says it's the best of both worlds, because she gets to learn lots of new things when she's researching the background to a book: add a touch of passion, drama and danger, a new gorgeous hero every time, and it's the perfect job!

Kate's always delighted to hear from readers, so do drop in to her website at www.katehardy.com

Previous titles by the same author:

THEIR CHRISTMAS WISH
THE FIREFIGHTER'S FIANCÉ
HIS HONOURABLE SURGEON
HER HONOURABLE PLAYBOY
HER CELEBRITY SURGEON

For Gerard, Chris and Chloë. Just because.

CHAPTER ONE

No. This couldn't be happening. Especially not today.

The back wheels fishtailed wildly, swinging the car from side to side before slamming it into the side of the kerb.

'No, no, no. You steer *into* the skid,' Lisa reminded herself loudly.

Problem was, she wasn't sure which way that was, because her car was still fishtailing down the hill. One thing she did know, you weren't supposed to brake hard on ice. You were supposed to take your foot off the accelerator and let the car slowly, slowly—

The jolt went right through her as the car hit the kerb again and bounced off.

OK. Calm down. Steer to the kerb. Stay in first gear. Let the car come to a halt.

One last bounce, and the car finally stopped.

And now she was stuck.

Couldn't stay where she was, because she was an obstacle—one that might cause someone else to have an accident as they tried to negotiate their way around her on the ice.

Couldn't go back—no way could she reverse up a hill that was covered in ice.

Couldn't go down—the hill loomed below her, a sheet of ice. If she slid across to the other side of the road, the chances were that she'd hit another car on its way up the hill. And she might not be able to stop at the bottom of the slope either, so she could end up driving straight into the path of an oncoming car. A car that wouldn't be able to avoid her on the icy road and would smash into the side of hers, the door buckling in and her body crushed.

Was this what had happened the day her father—?

No.

She wasn't going to think about that. Now

really wasn't the time. Or the place. She took her keys out of the ignition with shaking hands and put on her hazard lights.

This wasn't supposed to happen. Not in *March*. It was supposed to be the start of spring, for goodness' sake, not the depths of winter.

'Lisa Richardson, you can't wuss out of your first day in a new job,' she informed herself sternly. 'You're trained to winch out of helicopters. You're going to be clipping people into a safety harness when you're balancing on a tiny ledge above choppy seas. And that's a hell of a lot scarier than driving down an icy little hill.'

Except right now it didn't feel like it. Even her hands were stiff with panic and refused to grip the steering-wheel.

'All you have to do is drive to the bottom. You know the main road will be gritted. Just take it steady. It doesn't matter if you have a hundred cars behind you, wanting you to hurry up. Ignore any flashing lights or car horns. Just drive. Slowly. Get to the bottom of the hill. Turn right. Get on the main road out of the village and go to work,' she said loudly.

But the pep talk wasn't working. Every nerve-end was jangling at the thought of going down the hill, out of control. She could even see the smash happening in slow motion, hear the splintering glass and screeching of metal against metal. A sound that echoed back and back and back through her past.

I can't do this! I can't! she screamed mentally.

And then she screamed for real as she heard a bang.

It took her a couple of seconds—seconds that felt like hours—to realise that someone had knocked on the passenger window. All her windows had steamed up, so she couldn't see who it was.

She put the key back in the ignition, then pressed the button to lower the electric window until there was a gap of a couple of centimetres. Not enough for whoever it was to put a hand through—she wasn't that stupid—but enough to talk through.

'Are you all right?' a concerned male voice asked.

'Just hit some ice and smacked into the kerb. It caught me a bit on the hop.'

Oh, talk about sounding *wet*. She'd never

played the helpless female, batting tear-spiked eyelashes and wobbling her lower lip to get her own way, and she wasn't going to start now. And she certainly wasn't going to tell a complete stranger why she was so wussy about driving on ice. 'Sorry to block your way—I'll move in a second,' she said. And she fully intended to, once she'd psyched herself up to driving again.

There was a pause while he seemed to be inspecting her car. 'Looks as if you've cracked one of your wheel covers,' the voice informed her. 'Do you want me to follow you down the hill, just in case there's a problem?'

A problem? Did he think that the impact had damaged the wheel or her steering? Oh, no. A road covered in black ice was bad enough. Add dodgy steering, and she was a crash waiting to happen. A crash just like the one that had…

With an effort, Lisa pulled herself together. 'I'm sure it'll be OK.' She wasn't sure at all, but she needed to feel back in control. And sounding in control was the first step towards being in control, wasn't it? 'Thanks for the offer, though.'

The tremor in her voice must've been obvious,

because he said, 'You don't sound very OK. You're new around here, aren't you?'

No prizes for guessing that: her accent was pure south London, and right now she was in the northern part of Northumbria. Miles and miles and miles away. She dragged in a breath. 'Yup.'

'This road catches even locals unawares when there's a cold snap,' he said. 'The sun comes out for just long enough to melt the ice, then it freezes up again into what feels like a sheet of polished glass.'

He had a nice voice. Calm. Reassuring. It sounded as if he was smiling, and for a second she relaxed and smiled back. 'We don't really get icy roads like this in London.' It was always slightly warmer in the capital than it was else-where in the country. 'And I've never fishtailed down a hill before.'

'It's pretty scary, the first time it happens.' He ducked slightly, and she could just see his eyes through the gap in the window. Amazing eyes. A mixture of grey and gold and green, with unfairly long, dark lashes. Was the rest of him as beautiful as his eyes?

Though sitting in a car halfway down an icy hill was the last place she should start fantasising about a complete stranger. Even if the guy wasn't already committed elsewhere, a relationship didn't figure in her plans for the future. No way was she ever going to lose the love of her life and spend the rest of her days in the shadows, the way her mother had.

'Would it help if I drove your car down to the bottom of the hill for you?' he asked.

The coward in her leapt at the idea; she pushed it back. 'That's very kind of you, but I'll be OK.' Apart from the fact that Lisa had always handled her own problems, the man was a complete stranger. And common sense told her that you didn't let a strange man get in your car and drive you wherever he liked, even if he did have a nice voice and stunning eyes.

'If you're sure. I'll follow you for a bit. If you're worried about anything, just stick your hazard lights on and pull over, and I'll pull in behind you and sort it out.'

He'd definitely earned his Sir Galahad badge. 'Thanks.'

'No worries.'

A few moments later she took a deep breath, released the handbrake and crawled along the road. The car smacked into the kerb twice more, jolting her, but then she reached the bottom of the hill. To her relief, she managed to stop before the line. And as soon as she turned onto the main road she could feel that the surface had been gritted. No skiddiness. Everything was absolutely fine.

There was a red car following her: Sir Galahad from the hill. She flashed her hazard lights twice and gave him the thumbs-up sign to let him know that she was perfectly OK now. He imitated her sign—but a couple of miles later she noticed that he was still following her.

He was still behind her when she turned off towards the hospital.

And he was still behind her when she pulled into the car park.

Surely he should have turned off by now? Why was he still there?

Stop being stupid, she told herself sternly. Of course the man wasn't a stalker or some kind of maniac. He was just a stranger who'd spotted her looking as if she was in trouble—which she *had* been—and he'd been kind enough to make sure she reached her destination safely. He'd drive away again in a moment. She was still just a bit rattled from that horrible out-of-control feeling as she'd slid down the hill. Overreacting. Being silly.

But then he parked two spaces away from her. Too close for comfort.

Lisa took a deep breath and blew it out very, very slowly. So, what were her options? One, she could make a run for it and hope she made it through the hospital doors before he did. Two, she could face him down. Three, she could call the police.

Option one: the chances were, he'd be able to run faster than she could. So, no.

Option two: brave, but foolish.

Option three: and tell them what, precisely? That a man had parked two spaces away from her? *Pa-a-a-thetic.*

She went for option four. Stay still and see what he did next. She was in a locked car, so she was perfectly safe where she was.

Lisa pretended to be looking in her handbag

for something and waited, watching the red car out of the corner of her eye.

The door opened. The driver got out, shrugged a coat on and headed straight for the hospital entrance. He didn't even so much as glance in the direction of her car.

Her whole body went limp with relief—and embarrassment. How stupid had she just been? Convincing herself that her Sir Galahad had turned into a stalker. For goodness' sake! It was obvious that either he worked here or he was visiting someone.

And she'd better get a move on or she was going to be late. On her first day. Not good at all.

She grabbed her handbag and coat, locked the car door behind her and headed for the emergency department.

Ten minutes later Julie, one of the staff nurses, was showing Lisa around the ward. They were just passing the cubicles when a curtain twitched back and a doctor in a white coat emerged.

Lisa blinked hard. She recognised those amazing eyes from the gap above her steamed-up window. And the rest of him was even more gorgeous. Movie-star handsome—high cheek-bones, a strong jaw and sensual mouth that made you want to beg him to use it on you. Broad shoul-ders, narrow hips and capable hands. The kind of man women lost their heads over—big time.

She didn't think she'd ever seen such a beau-tiful man.

If he ever went out wearing a black poloneck sweater and black trousers, every woman who saw him would be a quivering puddle of hormones within seconds.

'Hey, Joel.' Julie smiled at him. 'Meet our new SHO, Lisa Richardson. Lisa, this is Joel Mortimer—he's our registrar.'

'Sir Galahad.' Lisa spoke without thinking.

Julie raised an eyebrow. 'Am I missing something?'

'He came to my rescue when I got stuck on some ice on the way to work this morning,' Lisa explained.

'Oh, right.' Julie smiled. 'That figures. Rescuing's what Joel does.'

Lisa's pulse missed a beat. Was he a volunteer

doctor with the air ambulance crew, too? Would she end up in a helicopter with him, sitting so close that their knees touched? Oh-h-h. Her temperature had just shot up ten degrees.

Before Lisa could embarrass herself by asking, Julie added with a grin, 'Though usually it's in his skimpy red trunks.'

Please, please don't let me be hyperventilating at the idea of a man this gorgeous wearing the skimpiest of clothes, his wet hair slicked back and his body glittering in the sun with droplets from the sea, Lisa begged silently.

Joel groaned. 'Don't listen to a word she says. I do *not* wear skimpy trunks. I'm a coastguard, not a lifeguard.'

Coastguard? Not part of the air ambulance crew, then. Lisa was shocked by the disappointment that surged through her.

'You wore a pair of skimpy red trunks for the charity auction,' Julie reminded him, laughing.

'Only because Beth nagged me into it. And that was *your* fault. You put the idea into her head in the first place, you horrible woman,' Joel informed her, smiling back.

Beth? His wife? Lisa glanced at his left hand— no sign of a wedding ring. Though maybe he just didn't wear one.

'I suppose at least you didn't wax your chest. Or bleach your hair and get a fake tan,' Julie teased.

Beautiful hair, Lisa thought. So dark it was almost black. Glossy, tousled curls which he'd clearly raked back with one hand, though a lock of hair flopped forward over his forehead. She suppressed the urge to reach forward and brush it back. Just.

'Thanks for stopping and helping me this morning,' she said awkwardly.

'No worries. You're not the first one who's been caught out on that hill, and you won't be the last. If I'd realised you were coming here, I could've offered you a lift,' he said with a smile.

And, lord, what a smile. It actually made her knees go weak.

Very, very bad. Joel Mortimer was definitely someone to stay away from.

'So you're a coastguard as well as a doctor?' she asked, hoping that her voice sounded completely normal—though she had a nasty feeling that she sounded breathless and a bit squeaky, like a schoolgirl asking her favourite pop star for an autograph.

He shrugged. 'As a volunteer. They call me if they need me.'

The air ambulance service here was run on a similar basis, staffed mainly by volunteers. In London, she'd been on secondment to HEMS for six months and had loved every minute of it. Here, the paramedics on the air ambulance crew were full time but the doctors volunteered to do a shift for a couple of days each month, on their off-duty. Lisa didn't mind working an extra two days a month for nothing: the way she saw it, she was putting something back in.

And maybe her work could stop someone else losing half their family, the way she had when she'd been sixteen.

'So what made you come to Northumbria?' Joel asked.

'I'd finished my stint at HEMS, so it was time to move on.' She shrugged. Why Northumbria? 'I came here on holiday with my parents when I was a kid.' It had been her last holiday with both parents. She'd just finished her GCSE exams, and although all of her friends had been planning to go on holiday together, travelling by rail through Europe for a month before settling down to start their A levels, her parents had asked her to spend that one last holiday with them instead of taking her first steps into the big wide world with her friends.

She'd been torn. If she didn't go to Europe with her friends, she'd miss out on swimming in St Tropez, eating the best ice cream in the world in Venice and being chatted up by gorgeous Greek waiters. And she'd feel that somehow she was a baby while all her friends had taken that extra step away from childhood.

But she adored her parents. And they weren't stuffy like most of her friends' parents. They talked to her as if she were an adult and her opinion mattered, that she wasn't just some silly little teenage girl.

In the end she agreed to go with her family. And after what happened barely six months later, she was so glad she had. That she'd not done the stroppy teenager bit and refused to hang out with her parents. That she'd enjoyed a holiday of simple English pleasures—the gardens at Alnwick where every breath you took was filled with the scent of roses, so strong that you could actually taste the flowers; poking round ancient castles and second-hand book-shops; walking along part of Hadrian's Wall and stopping off at little cafés to have stotties for lunch, the huge local bread rolls filled with cheese and ham.

Funny how memories so good could still hurt.

'I remember the beaches being amazing,' she said. 'These huge stretches of sand underneath cliffs with enormous castles.'

'The beach here is fabulous. And they sell the best fish and chips in the world on the harbour—you really have to try them.'

Was he offering…?

No. And she wouldn't have accepted, even if he'd asked. She didn't *do* relationships.

'Well, welcome to Northumberland General.' Joel held his hand out. Lisa took it, and was shocked to feel her fingers actually tingling. She couldn't remember the last time she'd responded that strongly to anyone.

But no way would a man as good-looking as Joel Mortimer be unattached. From what he'd said to Julie, Lisa knew that there was someone called Beth in his life—girlfriend, fiancée, maybe even his wife. Even if she broke her personal no-relationships rule, she'd never break up someone else's relationship to do that. She mentally hissed instructions to her libido to sit still.

'Better get on. My guess is we'll have a dozen Colles' fractures in this morning.' He shrugged. 'Always do when it's as icy as this.'

'People slipping on the path and putting their hands out to save themselves,' Lisa said. 'The record in my department in London was forty in a day.'

Julie whistled. 'Wow. Don't think I'd like to beat that. Come on, let me show you around the rest of the department, and then you can meet the team.'

'See you later,' Joel said. 'Enjoy your first day with us.'

'Thanks.' She smiled back, and let Julie lead her away from Joel.

Gorgeous. That was the only word to describe Lisa Richardson. In her car, her face white with fear, she'd looked beautiful but remote. There had been something almost other-worldly about her—an elfin face, huge blue-grey eyes and dark hair cut in a gamine, slightly spiky style that reminded Joel of Audrey Hepburn. Here, on the ward, she'd seemed warmer. Nearer. And when she'd shaken his hand, his skin had tingled at her touch. A tingle that had worked all the way down to the base of his spine. A tingle that had made him want to take her hand and trace a path with his mouth, starting at the pulse beating at her wrist up to her inner elbow and moving up to her shoulder, gliding along the sensitive cord at the side of her neck and then finally—

No. She might be the most attractive woman he'd met in a long, long time, but nothing was going to happen between them. There wasn't an official hospital rule banning relationships between staff on the same ward, but everyone knew it was a bad idea—they'd all had to work on a team where a personal relationship had shattered and soured the working relationship, too. Besides, Joel had learned his lesson the hard way. Relationships weren't his strong point.

She'd called him 'Sir Galahad'; he winced inwardly at the memory. You couldn't get much further from the truth than that. The gallant knight in shining armour who rescued maidens from peril. Ha. He hadn't been able to rescue the one person he *should've* been able to rescue. As knights in shining armour went, he was an utter failure. If that was how she saw him, he'd only end up disappointing her.

And then there was Beth.

No, it would be much too complicated.

He shook himself and strode to the reception area to find his next patient.

CHAPTER TWO

THE next week flew by, and Lisa was too busy to say more than hello to Joel. They weren't on the same shift pattern either: she'd seen him when she'd been on early shift and one of the lates, but not on the two nights she did in her first week.

Not that she asked why the registrar wasn't doing night shifts. It wasn't any of her business.

Particularly as she'd overheard a certain telephone call on the Thursday.

'OK, honey. I'll pick you up from Hannah's as soon as I finish here. See you soon. Love you, too, Beth.'

She shouldn't have listened. Or sneaked that look at Joel's face. Seen the softness of his eyes and the sheer love in his smile—the same expression she'd seen on her mother's face whenever she'd looked at Lisa's father.

True love.

The One.

And then, when it was all over, what then?

Her mother had had years and years and years of loneliness. Sure, of course she'd needed time to mourn the love of her life. Of course she wouldn't have wanted to find someone else straight away. But it had been so long—twelve years of being on her own, of nobody ever measuring up to The One. Lisa had promised herself she'd never, ever let herself fall in love with someone so deeply that he'd be her whole world and she'd never get over it if she lost him. And she'd kept that promise. She'd dated at med school, but she'd always kept things light. When her friends had started pairing off, she'd managed to avoid being set up with a suitable man by a shrug, a smile and the sweetly worded comment that you didn't need to date someone to have fun and she was doing just fine, thanks.

In the week she'd been here, Mark, one of the paramedics, had asked her out; so had the registrar on the maternity ward, Jack Harrowven. Lisa had turned them both down—though she'd gone out of her way to be charming in her refusal, and they'd agreed to stay purely friends and colleagues.

Which was just how it should be with Joel Mortimer. *Especially* as she knew he wasn't available.

Her body seemed to have other ideas and wasn't listening to the messages her brain was sending to it. Every time she caught his eye, there was a weird tingle at the base of her spine. Every time he spoke to her, her pulse sped up. Every time his hand brushed against hers when she handed over a set of notes or a piece of equipment, it felt as if an electric shock had gone through her. And it was wrong, wrong, *wrong*.

You, she told herself silently, need to get a life.

Starting tonight, when she was going out with the team for a Chinese meal.

The little boy's breathing was ragged, as if he was trying to hold back tears. Lisa glanced swiftly at his notes. She could still remember being nine and how uncool it was to cry, especially for boys. 'That looks painful,' she said gently. 'You're being very brave, Sam.'

'Yeah.' The word was clipped, as if he didn't trust himself to say any more. Didn't trust himself not to start howling.

He'd clearly hit the ground hard, at speed, because his sweatshirt was in ribbons. The skin beneath it was lacerated and studded with gravel—it would need proper irrigation or he'd end up with an infection. And Lisa didn't like the way he was nursing his arm. A dislocation at best—and a fracture at worst. Especially if the fracture involved the epiphyses, the growing ends of the long bones in the body, which could result in the growth plates fusing too early so the arm would be too short when Sam was fully grown. 'What happened?' she asked.

'Fell off my bike,' Sam muttered.

'Tell the doctor the truth,' his mother said, rolling her eyes.

'I fell off,' the boy insisted.

His mother sighed. 'And you're not getting any sympathy from me. I've told you before you're not to go near Mr Cooper's drive. And to wear elbow pads when you're on your bike. At least you had the sense to keep your cycling helmet on.' She looked at Lisa. 'We live in a cul-de-sac. The boys all race like mad down it and stop just before they hit the old man's drive at the end. It's some stupid game where they see who can stop the fastest and the nearest to the gravel. Half the time they come straight over the handlebars. The other half, they skid on the gravel and come off. Just like that.' She gestured to her son's arm. 'We've all told the kids not to do it—because it's not fair to the old man, having them scatter his gravel everywhere, as well as it being dangerous for them—but since when do little boys ever listen to their mothers?'

'I'm *not* a little boy. I'm almost a teenager,' Sam grumbled.

'You've got four years until you're a teenager. That isn't "almost",' his mother retorted. 'Now, let the doctor look at your arm.'

'It hurts,' Sam said between clenched teeth.

'I know, sweetheart, and I'll try to make it stop hurting very soon. Can you wiggle your fingers for me?' Lisa asked.

He did, but she noticed him flinching.

'Where did it hurt most?' she asked.

'My arm.'

Wrist? Elbow?'

'All of it.'

'I really need to examine your arm properly,' she said gently, 'because you might have broken something or dislocated a joint. But first I think we need to stop it hurting, and I'll also need to get all that grit out of your arm so it doesn't get really sore.'

'It hurts now.' His eyes widened as she stepped nearer. 'Don't touch it. *Please*, don't.'

She smiled at the boy. 'I could leave it so you can gross out all your mates with the pus that'll appear over the next day or so, but that'll hurt an awful lot more in the long run. Trust me, it'll hurt a lot less and heal much faster if you let me clean it properly now. What I'll do is numb the area first so you won't feel any pain.'

His eyes widened. 'You mean, you're going to stick a needle into me?' He dragged in a shaky breath. 'But they—they *hurt*!'

'He had a bit of a bad time when the nurse at

the surgery gave him his tetanus jab,' Sam's mother explained.

'Poor you,' Lisa said sympathetically. 'But I'm really good at this. I bet you won't even notice.'

'I will,' Sam said, and this time the tears came.

Oh, Lord. The poor kid really must be in pain: boys that age, in her experience, tried to tough it out as much as they could and hated to be treated as a baby. She had to do something—and fast.

'Hey.' She took his hand and squeezed it. 'I know injections can be scary. But I promise you, it won't hurt. And then all this pain in your arm will stop hurting, too. And did you know I have a special bravery certificate for boys who are being very, very brave like you are right now?'

'I want to go home,' he said, hiccuping through his sobs.

'Give him a cuddle,' she said softly to Sam's mother, 'and I'll be back in a tick.' She needed someone who was good at distracting—and that included the mum as well as the little boy. Lisa could understand the woman's exasperation, because she'd obviously told her son time and time again to be careful on his bike and he hadn't listened, but right now in her view Sam needed a cuddle more than a lecture. There would be time enough for telling him off later, when he'd stopped hurting.

Lisa twitched back the curtain, and nearly walked straight into Joel. She put both hands up in a gesture of apology. 'Whoops! Sorry. I wasn't looking where I was going.' Though she was very, very aware of his physical presence. Tall and strong and reliable.

'No worries. Everything all right?'

This was a very straightforward case and she really shouldn't be asking a registrar for help with it, but Joel was good at the Sir Galahad bit. And if he did coastguard rescues, he'd probably dealt with a lot of really frightened children— boys around Sam's age who went out on an inflatable full of bravado but then got trapped by the tide and ended up in tears.

And she'd just bet he'd be able to charm Sam's mum. No woman would be immune to a smile from a man this gorgeous.

She screwed up her nose. 'Have you got a minute, Joel?'

'What's up?'

She closed the curtain behind her and lowered her voice so her patient and his mother wouldn't hear. 'I've got a young lad who's fallen off his bike. His arm's a bit of a mess—and I'm not sure if he's broken or dislocated something. He's a bit chary about letting me look at it, and he's scared stiff of needles. I need something to distract him so I can get a proper look and work out if he needs an X-ray. And I could really do with getting the mum to stop nagging him.' She didn't dare tell Joel she wanted him to use his sex appeal on the mum—because that would be a dead give-away that *she* found him sexy. She'd concentrate on the little boy's needs. 'Are you good with kids, by any chance?'

Joel gave her an unreadable glance. 'You could say that.' Then the odd expression on his face vanished, and he smiled at her. 'Want me to come and talk him into letting us have a look?'

Oh, yes. That smile would *definitely* work on

Sam's mum. It had just made her own knees go weak. She nodded. 'Please.'

'OK. I'll distract him and you sort out the business end of the needle—assuming you're comfortable with that?'

'Sure. I'll use a fine needle—and I'll warm the local anaesthetic and buffer it.' That would help to make the injection less painful, and if Joel could keep Sam distracted she could inject the anaesthetic really slowly, which made it easier for children to tolerate. The last thing she wanted to do was make the little boy's fear of needles worse.

Joel followed her back into the cubicle and allowed her to introduce him to Sam and his mother.

Within seconds Joel had Sam laughing at a stream of silly jokes and had drawn him into talking about his favourite football team. Lisa prepared a syringe, waited for Joel's signal and swiftly eased the needle into place.

Sam was so busy telling Joel about the last football match he'd gone to with his dad he barely noticed what Lisa was doing. Gently she removed the needle and nodded to Joel.

'Right, then, Super Sam. Going to let us look at that arm now?' Joel asked.

'I...' The little boy went white. 'You're not going to put a needle in me now, are you?'

'No. Because I've already done it,' Lisa said quietly.

He stared at her, clearly surprised. 'But...but I didn't feel a thing!'

'Told you I was good at this.' She winked at him. 'I'm a doctor. I don't tell fibs. Any second now your arm's going to stop hurting.'

Sam's mother smiled in relief. Now Sam had stopped making a fuss, she seemed to have calmed down, too. Or maybe—as Lisa suspected—she'd been so stunned by how good-looking Joel was that she'd forgotten to be angry with her son. 'Thank you,' she said.

'That's what we're here for. Now, let's have a look at that arm.' Gently, Joel examined the boy and Lisa noted the way he was checking Sam's pulse and hand for any circulatory or neural problems. The discoloration of Sam's skin, the swelling and the odd angle of his arm made Lisa think the little boy had a fracture. Joel clearly thought so too because he said, 'I'm pretty sure you've broken your arm, so I'm going to send you for an X-ray to see what's happened.'

'Will it mean I have to have a plaster?' Sam asked.

'Yup. Though what sort of plaster depends on the type of fracture,' Joel said. 'And I need to know what sort of fracture it is before we can make it better. Do you know what an X-ray is?'

'Yes, we did it at school. It's like a camera and it shows your bones.'

'That's right. And the best thing is, it doesn't hurt,' Joel said with a smile.

'I'll get you booked in and clean up your arm while we're waiting for a free slot on the X-ray machines,' Lisa said.

'All right,' Sam said, perking up.

The local anaesthetic was working, she thought. Clearly the pain had eased, and Sam had turned from a sullen child into a chatty, interested little boy.

'Can I see my X-ray?' he asked.

'Of course you can. Do you think you might want to be a doctor when you grow up?'

'And have a white coat and stethoscope like yours? Mmm. I think I'd like to make people better. But not if someone's sick over me.' Sam pulled a face. 'It smells *disgusting* when someone throws up at school. The classroom stinks for ages afterwards. And it always looks like chopped carrots. Gross!'

Lisa laughed. 'I'm afraid we get quite a bit of that in here.' Particularly on Friday and Saturday nights, when people tended to overdo things in the pubs and clubs.

Sam looked disappointed. 'Oh. Maybe I won't be a doctor, then.'

'I'll be back in two ticks, when I've booked you in,' Lisa said, 'and then we'll get all the gunge out of your arm.'

Joel left the cubicles with her.

'Thanks for that,' she said. 'It really helped.'

'No worries.'

Just what he'd said when he'd rescued her on the hill. She smiled wryly. 'You seem to be making a habit of this.'

'Of what?'

'Rescuing me,' Lisa said. 'First on that hill,

now today when I needed help with a scared kid and a mum who'd lost her patience. I owe you.'

'Hey, everyone gets the odd case where they need help. We're a team here. Anyway, you'll probably return the favour by the end of the week. Kids I can do. Geriatric men—now, *they* loathe me.'

'Yeah, right,' she said with a grin. She couldn't imagine anyone loathing Joel Mortimer. There was just something about him: he was the sort men would want to be their friend and women would want to be their lover. Those gorgeous eyes... She could just imagine them, slightly hooded, looking at her across a crowded room. A private signal, telling her exactly what he was going to do when they were alone...

Oh, lord. She needed to get her thoughts under control. Fast. Joel wasn't free and she didn't do relationships anyway. And fantasising about the man who was practically her boss would definitely end in tears.

'Just call me if you need me,' Joel said.

Down, girl, Lisa scolded her libido silently. She wasn't going to make a move on Joel

Mortimer. Even if he did have the most beautiful eyes in the world and a sensual mouth that
made her quiver. 'Thanks,' she said, in the most
professional tones she could muster, and went to
book Sam's X-ray before she said something
really stupid to Joel.

She cleaned all the grit out of Sam's arm while
they were waiting for the slot in Radiology and
immobilised his arm in a sling. She asked for two
films—one lateral and one antero-posterior, both
including the joints and covering the entire
radius and ulna so she didn't miss any
problems—and was just checking them against
a lightbox when Joel came up beside her. 'How's
it looking?'

'Greenstick,' she said, showing him the section
on the X-ray where it was clear that one side of
the ulna shaft had bent while the other side had
broken. 'I'm just checking in case there's an
ephiphysal injury. It looks normal, but…'

'Worried about a Salter-Harris type V?' Joel
asked.

She nodded. With a Salter-Harris Type V
injury—also known as a crush injury to the

growing plate—the X-ray could look absolutely normal. It was notoriously difficult to diagnose the injury, but it had the greatest risk of causing the growth plates to fuse prematurely so the limb would always be too short.

'It's very rare,' Joel reassured her, his eyes narrowing as he looked at the films. 'And it's more common on the distal tibia. It's much more likely you'd find a Salter-Harris II fracture—' this was where the epiphysis separated from the bone, with a shape almost like a reverse tick '—but it looks as if he's been lucky.' He traced the outline of the cortex: a procedure Lisa had been taught to do as a house officer to make sure she didn't miss a subtle fracture by mistaking it for an ossification centre on the growing bone. 'Anything else you'd be worried about?'

'With an ulnar fracture, you need to check for a Monteggia fracture-dislocation,' she said. If you fell onto your ulna, as Sam had done, you could dislocate the head of the radius, the other main bone of the forearm, and the dislocation needed to be treated as well as the fracture. 'But there aren't any signs of it on the X-rays.'

'Agreed. This looks like a pretty straightforward case. What's your treatment plan?' Joel asked.

She didn't mind the questions, because she knew he was doing his job. She was his junior, he hadn't worked with her much, and he needed to know how competent she was—how far he could trust her to deal with patients on her own or whether she needed closer supervision. 'It's an angulated fracture, so I'll refer him to the orthopods for manipulation under a general anaesthetic. He'll have a cast on for a while, and I assume you have fracture clinics here in Paeds so I can get him booked in there for a follow-up.'

'Yup. Obviously you know what you're doing and you're sensible enough to ask if you need help. Carry on just as you are,' he said with a smile.

'Cheers.' Before she could stop herself, she added, 'Are you coming out with the team for the Chinese meal tonight?'

'No.' His voice was noticeably cooler. And he didn't offer an explanation, she noticed.

Not that she should expect one. He was a colleague—a senior colleague; he was barely an acquaintance, let alone a friend, and he didn't have to explain himself to her. Really, she shouldn't even have asked. It was none of her business.

'Um, I'll get back to my patient,' she said, and escaped back into the cubicle to show Sam his X-rays, as promised, and explain to him and his mother what was going to happen next.

Lisa didn't see Joel to speak to for the rest of the afternoon, and she'd put it out of her mind when she met the others at the local Chinese restaurant that evening.

'So how are you settling in?' Nell, the other registrar in their ward, asked Lisa.

'Fine.' Lisa smiled back at her. 'Everyone's really friendly, and I love my job.'

'So much that you volunteer for extra duties on your day off,' Julie said. 'On the air ambulance.'

Lisa blinked. 'Blimey. The hospital grapevine here's pretty fast, isn't it?' She hadn't said anything to anyone in the department, not wanting to sound...well...boastful. Setting herself up either as a heroine or a martyr. That wasn't where she was coming from at all. She had her own reasons for doing her rescue work—

reasons she didn't want to share. And she enjoyed doing it, too.

Julie chuckled. 'My boyfriend Marty's one of the full-time paramedics with the air ambulance. He saw your name on the list and asked me if I knew you. Your first duty's next week, isn't it?'

Lisa couldn't help smiling. 'Yes. I'm doing two slots a month. I'm really glad they accepted me, because I was on secondment to HEMS in London, and I loved every second of it. Though we could only do a six-month stint so we weren't over-exposed to trauma.'

'Rather you than me. I don't know how you do it.' Julie shivered. 'Winching out of a helicopter into thin air… No way would you get me doing that!'

'It's fine, once you get used to the idea,' Lisa said. 'You're perfectly safe. You're clipped into a harness, and when you go up with a stretcher, it's pretty smooth—you don't spin around on a rope and you don't even feel the downdraught from the blades. It's not like these action movies where you see someone hanging onto a ladder and blowing around madly in the wind.' She grinned. 'Oh, and you don't have all the baddies firing at you or have to dive through plate glass into a skyscraper, run out the other side and leap onto the rope ladder from several hundred feet up feet up.'

Julie laughed. 'Nope, you still haven't convinced me. I'd rather keep my feet firmly on the ground in the department!'

'If you're working with the air ambulance, you'll end up doing a rescue with the coastguard team at some point, then,' Ben, one of the other house officers, said to her.

'Not necessarily. You know as well as I do most of the work of the air ambulance is with RTCs or falls,' Julie said.

Not surprising, Lisa thought. Road traffic collisions, falls and suspected heart attacks were the most common reason for callouts in all the air ambulance services, usually in cases where it would take too long for a land ambulance to get through or the access to an accident site was poor.

'But Ben's right, we do get a few rescues on the cliffs and sea rescues. Joel'll introduce you to the coastguard team, if you ask him,' Nell suggested.

Lisa remembered what Joel had told her earlier. 'It's a bit unusual, a doctor being a volunteer coastguard.'

'It probably makes him feel he's giving something back,' Ben said quietly.

Lisa frowned. 'I'm not with you.'

'His wife died in an accident on the cliffs,' Nell explained.

It took a moment for it to sink in.

Joel wasn't committed elsewhere.

But he was so young to be a widower—he couldn't be more than in his early thirties. Obviously with his work on the coastguard team he was trying to make sure someone else didn't have to suffer the same kind of loss—just as she was, with the air ambulance.

Then she became aware that Nell was continuing. 'That's why he doesn't work nights or weekends.'

'Sorry, Nell. I didn't catch what you said. Joel doesn't do nights or weekends?' Lisa prompted.

'Childminders don't tend to do weekends and nights, and his parents are getting on a bit so they don't help out that much. Actually, to be honest, they were pretty hopeless when it happened,' Nell confided, 'and Vanessa's parents live the other side of the Pennines so they're no help either. Beth's a lovely kid but she can be a bit…well…demanding. As any kid would be when there's only one parent around.'

Oh. So Beth was Joel's daughter. And he was a single parent. Lisa flushed. 'Oh, no. I really put my foot in it today. I asked him if he was good with kids.'

'He is. And you weren't to know,' Ben said with a sympathetic smile.

'How old is she?' Lisa asked.

'Five. The accident happened a couple of years back.'

So Beth had been three when she'd lost her mum. It had been hard enough for herself at the age of sixteen, but three was so young. How tough it must be for Beth, seeing all her friends with a mummy and daddy—or even a step-parent—and wondering why she was different. 'Rough on her. Poor kid.'

'Yeah. But Joel's made it clear he's not looking for a mother figure for her,' Nell said.

'Warning received and understood,' Lisa said quietly. More than Nell would ever know. Because she understood exactly where Joel was coming from, too. She'd learned it well from her mother's example: nobody would ever match up to the man Ella Richardson had lost, and she'd loved him too much to want anyone else in her life.

Joel clearly felt exactly the same way about his late wife. So he was the last man on earth Lisa should want to get involved with.

'Joel's a lovely bloke. Salt of the earth. He'll do anything to help anyone. All I'm saying is, there's no point in any woman falling for him—gorgeous as he is—because no way will he let anyone into his life,' Nell said. 'Even though it would do him good.' She sighed. 'You can't live in the past. You have to move on, eventually.'

Ha. It had been twelve years, and Ella hadn't moved on. Lisa had the feeling that she never would. 'Some people just love one person too much to have room for anyone else,' Lisa said softly.

'Maybe.' Nell grimaced. 'Sorry, this is a bit of a miserable conversation for a Monday night.

Especially as we're supposed to be welcoming you to the team.' She topped up Lisa's glass. 'Ignore me. I didn't mean to imply that you'd throw yourself at him. I mean, you might be married.'

Lisa chuckled at the obvious fishing. 'Actually, I'm single. And that's the way I like it. I've got a career to think of.'

'Make sure you never sit in our receptionist's chair, then,' Ben warned darkly. 'Every woman who's sat there for the last three years has been married and off on maternity leave before you can blink!'

'Oi, you, don't start spreading rumours. I'm not pregnant,' Ally, the receptionist, called across the table. 'And I don't even have a boyfriend!'

Ben tapped the side of his nose with a forefinger. 'Just you wait. Give it six months, and you'll be getting your gran to knit you lots of bootees. That chair's got a reputation.'

Lisa laughed. 'Thanks for the warning. I'll remember that.' Though she wasn't planning on getting pregnant or even getting involved with anyone any time soon.

If ever.

CHAPTER THREE

'DADDY, you look growly,' Beth said.

Joel ruffled her hair. 'I'm fine, kitten.' Actually, he wasn't fine. Far from it. But he had no intention of worrying his daughter. 'Come on. Let's go to school.' Being on late shift meant that Beth was usually ready for bed when he picked her up from Hannah, her childminder, so he didn't get time for more than a bedtime story—and most of the time she fell asleep before he'd finished. But the good thing about late shifts was that instead of having to get her ready for school and dropping her off at Hannah's at the crack of dawn, he was able to take her to school himself. Which meant he saw her smiling, meeting her friends in the playground and running around with them, playing some sort of game or other.

He could see for himself that she was happy and well adjusted and settled.

Days like these, he thought maybe he was doing an OK job of being a single parent. That Beth was coping fine without having a mum.

And then the guilt would press down on him. Squash him flat. If he'd taken proper care of Vanessa in the first place…

Guilt that was doubly compounded by the X-rated dreams he'd had for the last week or so. Dreams about a certain SHO with an elfin face, mischievous blue eyes, straightforward manner and infectious smile. Dreams he had no right to have.

He certainly shouldn't have felt possessive when the coastguard crew had been discussing the new air ambulance doctor who'd attended the incident where a kid had got stuck in a hole when the tide had been on its way in, and how gorgeous she was. He shouldn't have wanted to snarl at them to leave her alone because she was already spoken for—by him. Because she *wasn't*. Lisa Richardson was a free spirit, someone who owed him nothing. Someone he couldn't expect to give up her single lifestyle and take on his commitments.

'Daddy?'

'Coming, sweetheart.' He managed to focus on his daughter until the classroom door opened, she kissed him goodbye and followed her schoolfriends inside. And then he stomped back to their cottage.

Why couldn't he get Lisa Richardson out of his head?

This was the first time in two years that any woman other than Vanessa had haunted his dreams. The first time in two years that he'd felt that pull of attraction. The first time in two years that he'd been aware of someone walking into a room even when his back was turned to the door.

But he couldn't let himself act on it. Couldn't take that risk again. It wasn't just his heart in danger: it was Beth's. And Lisa's, too, when he turned out to be Mr Wrong and let her down.

He blitzed the house, hoping that the action of scrubbing things clean again would scrub all thoughts of Lisa from his head. They'd worked together for a month, now, and although he thought she was a fine doctor—soothing the patients without being patronising, then treating them efficiently and effectively—she was completely wrong for him.

Number one, she worked in the same department, and inter-departmental relationships were always bad news for the rest of the team.

Number two, she could be engaged or even married, as far as he knew.

Ha. Who was he trying to kid? Ben had already mentioned that Lisa was available. And that she'd turned Jack Harrowven and Mark down when they'd asked her out. And he really shouldn't have been quite so pleased about that.

Number three… Oh, come on. Surely he could think of a third reason. He should be able to think of a *dozen* reasons why seeing Lisa would be a bad idea. Between Beth, work and the coastguard, there wasn't any room for a relationship in his life.

And it was completely irrelevant that he saw Lisa at work and sometimes when he was volunteering. On her last duty on the air ambulance, he'd actually worked with her: he'd helped her strap a casualty into a stretcher and checked her line before she'd been winched up from his lifeboat.

He scrubbed harder at the limescale in the shower. He was *not* going to think about Lisa Richardson. Or speculate how soft her skin might be. Or wonder how it would feel to have that beautiful mouth tracking down his body...

But it didn't work. He just couldn't get her out of his head. So he was still in a bad mood by the time he started his shift.

A mood that worsened by mid-afternoon, when he was called to see a patient who'd been in a car accident and was complaining of abdominal pain. A patient who was six months pregnant: just like Vanessa had been when she'd died.

Part of him was tempted to give the case to someone else, someone who could cope with this sort of situation without any memories to cloud their judgement. But then his training kicked in. He was a senior doctor in the department. This was his *job*. He had to keep his emotions separate. Memories and sentiment had no place in an emergency department. He had to focus on the people who needed him. His patients.

He walked into the cubicle. 'Mrs Patterson?'

The woman on the bed was shaking uncontrollably. He sat down on the edge of her bed and took her hand. 'I'm Joel Mortimer, the registrar in the department. Can you tell me what happened?'

'I was in traffic. In a queue, waiting for someone to turn right. And someone rammed straight into the back of me.' She dragged in a breath. 'And now—now I can't feel my baby moving. And my stomach hurts. And I'm wet—between…' She shuddered. 'Between my legs,' she whispered. 'But it's too early. My waters can't have broken yet. They just *can't*.'

'Try not to worry too much until I've examined you,' Joel said gently. 'Babies are pretty hardy, and they're fairly well cushioned inside you. Does it hurt anywhere else?' He was half expecting her to describe whiplash injuries.

'No, just my stomach.'

Could be panic. But if her stomach had hit the steering-wheel and the wetness was blood…

Joel had a bad feeling about this. At the handover the paramedics had mentioned impact against the steering-wheel: not hard enough to trigger the airbag, but clearly hard enough to have hurt Mrs Patterson. He had a nasty feeling this could be a placental abruption—and a bad tear could be an emergency for the mother as well as the baby.

'I'm going to examine you, if that's all right with you, and meanwhile I'll get a portable scanner brought in so we can take a look at the baby and see what's going on.' And, please, please, it would be just panic that was making her unable to feel the foetal movements. He'd do an ultrasound and the baby would be visible on screen, kicking away as if nothing had ever happened.

'Don't let me lose my baby,' Mrs Patterson begged. 'Please, don't.'

If it was a major abruption, there might not be much choice. Not at twenty-six weeks. Very pre-term babies could survive in Special Care, but often it took months and months of heartache and worry, and the babies were often left with long-term problems. His heart ached for her. 'We'll do our best for you,' Joel promised. 'I'm going to order that scanner. I'll be back in three minutes, tops. Start counting the seconds—I want you to take a big breath in while you say "one second" in your head, and then a big breath out while you say "one second". Can you do that for me?' He knew from experience that counting breaths would help to calm her, and concentrating on a simple task would help to distract her from her panic.

She nodded, and began to take deeper, longer breaths.

'That's perfect,' Joel said with an encouraging smile. He was gone for just long enough to ask one of the staff nurses to get him a scanner, page the maternity registrar and order four units of O-negative blood as a matter of urgency, and then went straight back to Mrs Patterson.

'I'm going to examine you now,' he said gently. 'Just tell me if anything's uncomfortable or if you need me to stop. Don't worry about being embarrassed or feeling silly—I'm here to look after you, and how you're feeling is the most important thing right now.'

But he wasn't happy with what he saw. Mrs Patterson had a small vaginal bleed—the blood was dark red and clotted—but she was starting to look slightly shocky, out of proportion to the amount of blood she'd lost. Her blood pressure was low, too. All the signs were pointing to a placental abruption—the impact from the car accident could have caused part of the placenta to tear away from the wall of the uterus. In cases of minor placental abruptions, the patient could often go home to rest and the tear would repair itself over the next few days. But with a major placental abruption, it could mean an immediate Caesarean section in an attempt to save the mother's life as well as that of the baby.

Joel had a really bad feeling about this one.

Particularly when he couldn't hear the baby's heartbeat either.

Maybe the baby was lying awkwardly and that was why he couldn't pick up the heartbeat. But he'd feel a hell of a lot better when the portable ultrasound scanner arrived and he could see what was going on. Not to mention having the obstetric specialist on hand.

'Is my baby all right?' Mrs Patterson asked, her voice rasping and shuddery with fear.

He didn't want to panic her. But he didn't want

to lie either. 'Try not to worry,' he said softly. 'I'm going to chase that scanner.'

To his relief, Jack Harrowven, the senior registrar from the maternity unit, was already walking into the department. Joel took him to one side and gave him a quick rundown on the case. 'I think it's an abruption. A big one. We're waiting for the portable scanner, but I can't hear the baby's heartbeat.'

'Oh, hell,' Jack said. 'Doesn't sound good.'

'It might be the way the baby's lying,' Joel said.

Jack shook his head. 'If the mum can't feel movement either, that's not a good sign.'

Joel took a deep breath, showed Jack to Mrs Patterson's cubicle and introduced him to the patient. The scanner arrived at the same time.

'Please. Don't let my baby die,' Mrs Patterson begged again.

'We'll do our best,' Jack said. 'Can you pull your top up a little bit for me? I'm going to put some gel on your stomach, and then we'll see what's happening.'

'Mrs Patterson, I've been called to see another patient,' Joel said, 'but I'm leaving you in the best possible hands. Jack's the best obstetrician I know.' He smiled at her. 'He delivered my daughter.'

Though as he left he glanced at the screen. And what he saw told him that even an obstetrician as good as Jack wouldn't be able to do much.

Ah, hell. He knew all about how bad it felt to lose a baby at six months' gestation. Vanessa hadn't survived the accident. And neither had Beth's little brother: at twenty-four weeks, he'd been just too tiny.

Life, he thought savagely, really *sucked* sometimes.

'You all right?' Lisa asked when he almost walked straight into her in the corridor.

'Fine,' he lied, his voice clipped.

'You don't look it. Bad case?' Without waiting for an answer, she added, 'Why don't you take five minutes, have a coffee or something?'

Because he needed to keep busy. If he took five minutes, right now, he'd remember far too much. Feel the pain rolling over him yet again. Get sucked back into the dark days. He couldn't afford that to happen. Not here, not now, not ever. He gritted his teeth. 'Thank you, Dr

Richardson, but I take orders from my consultant, not my SHO.'

Her eyes widened with hurt. 'But I wasn't ordering you. It was just a suggestion because you look a bit…well…' Her voice trailed off.

'I'm perfectly fine, thank you. Now, if you'll excuse me, I have patients to see.' He brushed her aside and strode off, aware that he was behaving appallingly but unable to stop himself. Right now he was way, way too close to the edge.

Later that afternoon, the news filtered through the department that Mrs Patterson had lost her baby. As soon as Lisa realised that Mrs Patterson had been Joel's patient, she could guess why Joel had looked so rattled. And why he'd bitten her head off. Cases where babies or children didn't make it were always hard, but even more so for doctors and nurses who had children of their own—and that was intensified for single parents. Lisa didn't know the details of Joel's wife's accident, but if it had been in a car this had probably reminded him of it.

She hated to think of him sitting in his office,

dealing with paperwork and just hurting. Being buffeted by memories. She'd been there often enough. Every time she had to attend a traffic accident with the air ambulance, or dealt with the fallout in Resus, the memory knifed through her for an instant before she pushed it away, reminded herself that she was a professional and dealt with the case. It must be just as tough for Joel. Tougher, really, because it had only been a couple of years ago; she'd had twelve years to get used to her own loss.

On impulse, when her shift finished, she went over to his office and knocked on his door.

'Yes?'

His tone was still slightly curt, but she ignored it and walked in. Closed the door behind her.

He looked at her, not smiling. 'What can I do for you, Dr Richardson?'

He'd still got that barrier up between them, then. Until this afternoon he'd called her by her first name. They had been a *team*. Well, she wasn't going to let him put her off now. When she had moments like these, she really needed other people around her. Someone to pull her back from the fear. 'I wondered if you'd like a coffee or anything, Joel.' She deliberately used his first name.

'No, thanks. I'm catching up with my paperwork.'

And the look he gave her said very clearly that she was holding him up. 'When you've finished, then. Maybe we can go for a drink or something.' And maybe he'd talk to her. Talking had always helped her in the past.

He frowned. 'A drink? Lisa, you need to understand I'm not in the market for a relationship.'

He thought she was asking him out? She scoffed. 'Actually, I wasn't asking you for a relationship. I was asking you out as a colleague who can see you've had a rough day—the kind of day when it might help to talk to someone who understands. I meant a *drink*, as in coffee or something. Nothing else.'

'Oh.' He didn't apologise, though colour slashed across his cheekbones so clearly he knew he was in the wrong. 'Sorry, I need to be somewhere.' He glanced at his watch. 'Like now.'

Of course. His little girl. She should have thought. 'Sorry. I shouldn't have held you up. Goodnight.'

Lisa had closed the door behind her before Joel had a chance to say anything. He groaned and covered his face with his hands. He'd been a first-class bastard, snapping at her and leaping to conclusions—stupid conclusions. Of *course* she hadn't been asking him out. She'd just seen him as a colleague who'd had a rough day and wanted to make him feel better. He'd been projecting his own thoughts onto her—his own ridiculous desire for a relationship with her.

And he'd overreacted. Big time. Had pushed her away as hard as he could, because there was something about Lisa Richardson that made him really want her. And he wasn't in a position to offer her any sort of relationship.

Ah, hell. He'd apologise tomorrow. Explain that the case had brought back memories for him and he shouldn't have taken it out on her.

Though wild horses wouldn't drag from him the fact that he'd pushed her away for another reason—to keep temptation at bay.

He saved the file he'd been working on and shut down the computer, then headed for Hannah's to pick up Beth. She fell asleep in the car, as she always did when he was on a late shift; he carried her to bed, tucked her in, and stood watching her for a moment. Sometimes she looked so like Vanessa when she was sleeping that it hurt.

But he'd never let his daughter down the way he'd let his wife down. She'd come first in his life. Always.

The next morning, he dropped Beth at Hannah's, then made a swift detour into the hospital shop on his way to the department. Flowers? No. Too ostentatious. And it might give the wrong message. He wanted something that said sorry in a colleague-like fashion.

Every medic he knew loved chocolate. So it was a pretty safe bet.

He bought the nicest box the shop had, then headed for his office, grabbed a sticky note from his desk and scribbled her a quick note. *Sorry. Bad day yesterday. Shouldn't have taken it out on you. Cheers, Joel.*

Yep. That would do. It sounded like a note from a colleague, not a lover.

Lover.

Nope, he had to push that word right out of his head. He wasn't going to be Lisa's lover. No matter how much his body wanted him to.

He went swiftly to the restroom. Her locker was—of course—locked. Great. He knew she was never late for her shift—that meant she had to be on a late shift. He'd try to catch her just before she started, then. With a sigh he returned to his office, shoved the chocolates in a drawer, then went out to see the night staff for the handover to his shift.

Facing Joel was something Lisa really didn't want to do. She'd spent most of the previous night feeling hideously embarrassed. He'd actually thought she'd been asking him out on a date. That she fancied him.

The worst thing about it was, he was right. She *did* fancy him. She just wasn't going to do anything about it. Because she had a feeling that, if she let him, Joel Mortimer could be very, very important in her life. And she wasn't going to make her mother's mistakes. Wasn't going to love someone so much that the world stopped without them.

She'd just changed her shoes and locked her locker door when Joel strode into the restroom, his hands behind his back. He looked like one of the consultants you saw on TV dramas, ordering a junior doctor, 'Walk with me,' so he could explain some esoteric procedure or other. Cool and distant and clever.

'Morning,' he said.

'Morning,' she replied coolly.

'Lisa—look, I owe you an apology. I was incredibly rude to you yesterday. You were being kind, a good colleague, and I…' He grimaced. 'Well, I shouldn't take out my personal problems on my team.'

Oh, lord. Just when she'd been prepared to be an ice queen, he said something to melt her. The more so because he was so obviously sincere.

He coughed. 'Um—this is by way of an apology.' He drew his hands from behind his back and handed her a large brown paper bag.

She peered inside, and smiled. 'You didn't need to do that, Joel—but thank you. Apology accepted. And if you're going to give me chocolates every time you have a bad day, I could be tempted to send every male geriatric who walks into the department your way.'

He laughed, clearly remembering that he'd told her elderly male patients loathed him. 'Just you try it. I'll make you deal with the really gory stuff.'

'I can do gory.' She'd attended enough accidents with the air ambulance in the past. She smiled. 'But I could do with learning a few of those bad jokes of yours for the next time I get a nine-year-old who needs distracting.'

'Done.'

Lord, he was gorgeous when he smiled. That slight quirk to his mouth, the crinkle at the corner of his eyes and the way his eyes turned almost pure gold. It made her want to reach out, touch his face. Run her thumb along his lower lip.

What would it be like to slide her fingers through those black, glossy curls and draw his head down to hers? Would his face be smooth, or would there be the faintest hint of stubble grazing against her fingertips as she stroked his skin? How would it feel when he kissed her—when his mouth brushed against hers, exploring, teasing, inciting, demanding a response?

It would be so easy to find out. All she'd have to do would be to slide her hand behind his neck and draw his face down to hers, brush her mouth against his and—

No. He'd made it clear they were just colleagues. She needed to get herself back under control. Like now. 'I'd, er, better show my face at Reception. Thanks again for the chocolates.'

'Pleasure.'

And she escaped before she did something *really* stupid.

Like kissing him.

CHAPTER FOUR

FOR the next week or so, Lisa managed to keep herself strictly professional when Joel was around. But then Friday turned out to be the sort of day when it seemed that everyone who couldn't get in to see their GP before the weekend decided to come to the emergency department instead. Lisa was on an early shift, but the waiting room was still full when she was due to go off duty.

'We're really snowed under and they're all grumbling about waiting. Would you be an angel and see one last patient before you go?' Ally, the receptionist, asked, looking hassled.

It wasn't as if Lisa had anything more pressing lined up than a workout at the gym, a long bath and then a good film. It wouldn't matter if she stayed a bit later. 'Sure,' she said with a smile, and took the proffered notes.

She saw several patients; when the queue had started to die down, she was finishing her paperwork and thinking about leaving when she overheard Ally saying, 'I'm sorry, Dr Mortimer's with a patient. I'll get a message to him as soon as I can.'

'When can I see him?'

'It depends on the patient,' Ally said. 'Please, take a seat. I'll call you as soon as I can.'

'But I need to see Joel *now*,' the woman insisted. 'It's really important.'

There was a note of almost panic in the woman's voice. It sounded as if something was wrong, and maybe Joel was the only doctor she trusted.

Lisa could understand that. When she'd been panicking on the icy hill, Joel had been the one to calm her down. But rescuing was what she was trained to do, too. Maybe she could help.

She walked over to the reception desk. 'Excuse me, I couldn't help overhearing you just now. I'm one of Joel's colleagues. Can I help at all?'

The woman shook her head. 'Thanks, but I have to see Joel.'

Desperation etched the other woman's face and Lisa felt for her. 'I'll see what I can do. Can I give him any idea what it's about?'

The woman sagged with relief. 'My mum's ill. I need to get over to her right now and I can't take Beth with me. Joel was meant to be collecting her. It's not usually a problem if he's late or he's been called out on a shout, but right now…'

Beth.

Lisa noticed the little girl standing next to the woman, holding her hand. A very feminine version of Joel, albeit with stunning deep blue eyes and a rosebud mouth she'd probably inherited from her mother. The rest of her colouring was pure Joel—alabaster skin and long near-black hair pulled back in a neat ponytail. She was still wearing her school uniform; she was biting her lower lip and shuffling from foot to foot, clearly feeling she was a nuisance. Lisa's heart went out to her.

'Look, Joel's probably not going to be that long.' He'd been due off shift at the same time as she had been—a good hour ago. 'I'll sit with Beth, if you like, until he's free.'

The woman looked torn between gratitude and reluctance.

Lisa smiled and proffered her ID card. 'I'm Dr Lisa Richardson. And I won't run off with young Beth. Ally'll vouch for me—won't you, Ally?'

The receptionist nodded. 'Course I will.'

'Well, if you're sure.' The woman still looked doubtful.

Lisa crouched down so she was at eye level with the little girl. 'Beth, my name's Lisa and I work with your daddy. Would you like me to read you some stories while your daddy's making somebody better?'

Beth nodded shyly.

The woman paused for a moment, then sighed. 'Thank you. Beth, your daddy will be here soon. Be good for Dr Richardson, OK?'

Beth nodded again, then bit her lip. 'Hannah, is your mummy going to die like mine did?'

Hannah must be the childminder, Lisa thought. And she looked very close to tears: clearly she was worried sick about her mother.

'Hey, not everyone dies when they're poorly,' Lisa said gently. 'Doctors can do a lot to make people better. That's what your daddy does.'

'He couldn't make my mummy better,' Beth said, matter-of-factly.

Ouch. 'But he makes lots of people better,' Lisa said.

'My mum's not going to die,' Hannah said. 'She's just not very well and I have to go to her.'

Lisa smiled at her. 'Don't worry. I'll look after Beth until Joel's free. She'll be fine with me.' She stood up and held her hand out to Beth. 'Shall we go and wait in your daddy's office?' It would be quieter there, and the little girl would be protected from any traumatic scenes in the reception area.

Beth nodded.

'Ally, when Joel comes out, can you tell him where we are, please?'

'Sure,' Ally said with a smile.

'OK, Beth. Let's choose a story.' She let Beth pick a couple of books from the box in the reception area, collected her handbag from her locker, then led the little girl through to Joel's office. She read the story, encouraging Beth read some of the easier words and talking through the pictures with her. As they neared the end of the book, Beth became less shy with her and eventually remarked, 'Your hair's really spiky.'

Lisa smiled. 'Yes. Short hair makes life easier at work. But when I was your age, I had long hair like yours.'

'Did you have a ponytail, too?'

Lisa nodded. 'Though sometimes my mum used to put it in plaits before I went to bed, so it was wavy the next day.'

'That's what Emma's mum does,' Beth said. Then her face fell. 'Daddy can't do plaits. Hannah doesn't have time and Grandma never does my hair.'

Knowing she really shouldn't be interfering but unable to stop herself making the offer, Lisa said, 'Would you like me to put your hair in plaits for you?' Surely two minutes braiding a little girl's hair wouldn't do any harm?

Beth's eyes widened. 'Oh, yes, please! Can you do princess plaits?'

'What are princess plaits?' Lisa queried.

'The ones that look like a crown.' Beth demonstrated a narrow arc round her head with her fingers and thumbs.

'Oh, the ones where you do just the front bits of your hair in a plait and clip them together at the back?' At Beth's nod, Lisa smiled. 'Sure I can.' Gently, she removed the hairband from Beth's ponytail, then took the comb from her handbag, combed her hair and quickly sorted out the plaits, fastening them together at the back with the hairband. She took the little compact mirror from her handbag and showed Beth. 'What do you think? Are they all right?'

'Oh, yes! I look just like a princess! Oh, thank you.' The little girl hugged her. 'I like you. You're nice. Do you know, that's my favourite hairband? Because it has a blutterfly on it.'

'A butterfly?' Lisa asked.

Beth nodded emphatically. 'A blutterfly,' she repeated.

Lisa smiled, charmed by the mispronunciation. 'It's lovely.'

'Do you know any songs about blutterflies?' Beth asked.

'No, but I know a good one about frogs.' One

her goddaughter had taught her, back in London. 'Do you know the one about the speckled frog sitting on the speckled log?'

Ten minutes later Joel stood outside his office door, hearing his daughter singing songs. She sounded perfectly happy, and his worries faded.

Not that he'd actually had anything to worry about. He already knew Lisa was good with children. Apart from her wobble during her first week in the department, that was—but everyone needed time to settle in. She'd more than proved herself a valuable asset to the team.

And Hannah couldn't help her mother's illness. She'd been well for a while, but the problem with bipolar was that it was a chronic condition, one that would flare up every so often. There would be a short crisis, and she'd need Hannah until she was back on an even keel again.

Until the next time.

It was his fault, too. He should've been off shift a long, long time ago and collected his daughter. But sometimes he forgot he should be Daddy first and doctor second. Forgot that there wasn't anyone else there to take up the slack when he was busy.

'Hello, kitten.' He leaned against the doorjamb. 'Thank you for looking after her for me, Lisa.'

'No worries,' Lisa said quietly.

'Lisa's been teaching me songs,' Beth said. 'And, look, she gave me a special princess torch.'

A pink one, which she waved with the glee you only saw on a five-year-old girl's face when she had something new and pink.

'And I can put glitter on it. Lisa was going to put glitter on hers, 'cept the glitter might fall off like it does on my pictures and make someone ill.'

Joel looked at Lisa. 'You really sh—' he began.

'It was a promotional freebie,' Lisa cut in. 'And I have more than one.'

'Even so. Beth, have you said thank you?'

'Of course I have.' She looked indignant. 'I have very good manners—haven't I, Lisa?'

Lisa chuckled. 'Yes, sweetheart, you do.'

Lord, Lisa was beautiful when she laughed like that. Such perfect white teeth. And soft, sweet, unpainted lips that made him want to dip his head down to hers and—

No.

He dragged himself back to the present, and was horrified to hear his daughter say, 'Why don't you have tea with us? We're having pasta tonight 'cos it's Friday and Daddy always makes pasta on Fridays. It's my favourite. *And* we're having garlic bread.'

Beth was inviting Lisa to dinner? Oh, help. He could just about stay professional at work. At home… No, it would be too much temptation. He really dared not risk it. 'Lisa's a busy lady,' Joel cut in swiftly. 'She won't have time.'

Her expression was unreadable. 'Yes, I have to go home now, Beth.'

'But you'll see me again soon?'

'Sure.' She dabbed the tip of her finger against the little girl's nose. 'Next time, *you* can teach *me* a song.'

'Thank you for looking after me,' Beth said, sliding off Lisa's lap.

'I enjoyed it.' Lisa winked at her, gave Joel a brief smile and left his office.

'She's really nice,' Beth said.

Yeah. He knew that.

'She's my friend. I like her.'

Me, too, Joel thought. In fact, I have a nasty feeling that I more than like her. That friendship wouldn't be enough—but I can't offer her anything more. Better to keep it strictly professional between us. 'OK, kitten,' he said, picking Beth up and giving her a hug. 'So have you had a nice day?'

'Yes. Look, Lisa did proper princess plaits in my hair, just like Emma's mum does,' Beth said, patting her hair.

Joel winced inwardly. He was depriving his daughter of a mother figure. He knew that. Hannah, bless her, did a good job but at the end of the day it was still a job—Beth wasn't her daughter. His mother didn't have the patience to deal with a little girl. And Beth was definitely missing out.

But he couldn't give her a mother. Look at the mess he'd made of his marriage. Who was to say it wouldn't happen again? Even if by some chance Lisa felt that same attraction, wanted to make a go of it with him, she'd soon find out all his flaws. How useless he was at reading people's feelings and moods. How, despite his best intentions, he put his job first.

And then she'd go.

And Beth's heart would be broken, as well as his own.

Beth had had enough unhappiness in her short life. He wasn't going to put her through the misery of trying to find a mum, someone who'd care for her and stay married to him.

'Your hair looks lovely. Now, shall we go home and make the pasta?' he asked, hoping that it would steer his daughter away from the subject of Lisa Richardson.

'Ooh, yes!' Beth said, hugging him. 'I'm really hungry.'

Me, too, Joel thought. Though this particular hunger wasn't one he'd be able to sate.

CHAPTER FIVE

'WHEN are you coming up to stay with me? Bring Monty—he'll love it, too.' Lisa could imagine her mother's dog running along the beach, wagging his tail happily and splashing through the waves. 'I'm dying to show you the beaches. Just miles and miles of sand. And there are castles everywhere. It's just...' Lisa glanced around her and sighed happily. 'Oh, it's just fabulous. You'll love it.'

'Is that where you are now, love?' Ella asked. 'The beach?'

Lisa could hear the laughter in her mother's voice and knew exactly why her mother was so amused. 'Yes,' she admitted. 'And, yes, I've got my jeans rolled up and I'm walking barefoot at the edge of the sea.' She'd always loved holidays by the sea as a child, and whenever she needed time to think, she headed for the sea. A walk along the shoreline, even in the depths of winter, always helped her see things more clearly. The wind blew the cobwebs away, the soft hiss of the sea against the shore soothed her, and the coolness of the water was like balm to her soul.

She'd been walking on the beach when she'd decided to make the move and apply for the job in Northumbria. Her friends had said she was crazy, making a sideways move. But the way she'd seen it, she hadn't been ready yet for a registrar's post. She'd have as much chance of promotion in Northumbria as she did in London; plus it meant she could still work with the air ambulance, doing the part of her job she loved best.

'You're paddling in the sea. The North Sea,' Ella said dryly. 'Which is freezing even in the middle of summer, let alone in late April.'

'It's invigorating,' Lisa corrected with a grin. 'I'm so glad I moved here, Mum. It was a good idea.' Even though she'd had a few doubts at the time. She'd always lived in London and Northumbria was at the other end of the country, several hours' drive away from her mother.

'You certainly sound a lot happier,' Ella commented.

'Course I'm happy, Mum. The department's great, so's the air ambulance team, and I love being so near to the sea.' The only thing missing was her family. But she could always bunch her off-duty together and drive down to London to spend a few days with her mum; in the meantime, the phone would have to do.

'Daddy, Daddy! Look, it's Lisa,' Beth said, tugging her father's hand and pointing at the woman who was paddling at the edge of the sea and talking animatedly into a mobile phone.

So it was, Joel thought.

And she looked very different away from work. In the department she usually wore smart black or navy trousers, a formal white or cream top and a white coat; there, she looked every inch the professional, caring doctor. Right now she was wearing a hot pink long-sleeved T-shirt and jeans rolled part way up her legs, leaving her slender ankles and feet visible. Faded jeans that clung lovingly to every curve. Soft, well-worn denim that made him want to touch, slide his hand over the fabric and then under her T-shirt, across her bare skin and drift upwards, before touching her more intimately…

Uh. He was with his *daughter*. He was meant to be looking after her, not going into a lust-hazed dream about his senior house officer. His junior. Someone he had to work with. This was a really, really bad idea.

But still he couldn't help watching Lisa. Her shoes were dangling from one hand, and she looked carefree and much, much younger than the twenty-eight years he knew her to be.

When had he last danced through the lapping waves like that, simply having fun and enjoying life?

He couldn't remember.

'Let's go and see her,' Beth said, bouncing beside him.

'She's busy talking to someone,' Joel reminded her. Lisa was still talking and smiling and laughing and looking out to sea; clearly she hadn't noticed them.

'But I'm sure she'd like to talk to us, too. She

hasn't seen us.' Beth waved her bucket and spade frantically at Lisa in an attempt to get her attention, and her bottom lip wobbled when it didn't work. 'Daddy, *please*.'

That earnest blue gaze, so like Vanessa's, the pleading smile—how could he resist? 'We'll walk towards her,' Joel said, 'but if she's busy talking to someone, we're not going to interrupt. All right?'

'Oh, yes,' Beth said happily. 'You're the best daddy in the world.'

He wasn't convinced of that, but he responded, 'And you're the best daughter in the world.' He meant every word. Beth was the light of his life, and he really didn't deserve her.

As they drew nearer to Lisa, he heard her say, 'Love you, too,' and was shocked by the dismay that surged through him.

It shouldn't matter if she was seeing someone else after all. It wasn't any of his business if she was seeing someone else. He came as part of a package, and he'd already overheard Lisa say that she was young, free and single and intending to stay that way. After that, he'd decided he definitely wasn't going to make a move. It wasn't fair to be dog in the manger about her. She deserved someone who wasn't weighed down with a ton of emotional baggage and a young family.

'Lisa! Lisa!' Beth yelled, before Joel had a chance to remind his daughter not to interrupt when people were speaking.

Lisa turned to face them and smiled back at the little girl. 'Call you later,' she said into the phone, and switched it off. 'Well, hello. Fancy seeing you here,' she said to Beth.

'We come here a lot,' Beth confided. 'Daddy used to be a lifeguard here before he was a doctor.'

A lifeguard in skimpy red trunks: Lisa remembered Julie's teasing in the department on her first day. And she had to suppress the desire that shimmered through her at the image of Joel, barefoot, with wet hair, his body glistening with drops of seawater, wearing only a pair of red swimming trunks…

Oh-h-h.

That hadn't been what he'd worn on the occasions when her helicopter had been out on the same rescue as his boat. Then he'd either been in the same kind of clothes he'd worn at work or—on one particularly memorable occasion— a pair of faded denims and a black poloneck sweater. Looking so incredibly sexy that she'd wanted to grab him and kiss him stupid. Only the fact that she'd had a patient to look after had stopped her making a fool of herself.

'You were a lifeguard?' she said to Joel.

'When I was in my late teens.' He shrugged. 'A long time ago.'

She laughed. 'You're not *that* old, Joel.' She turned to the little girl. 'So you like coming to the beach, do you, Beth?'

'It's my favourite place in the whole wide world,' Beth said.

'Mine, too,' Lisa said. 'When I lived in London, a day at the beach was my best treat ever.'

'And now you live here, you can come to the beach every day.'

Lisa smiled. 'When I'm not at work, yes— actually, I do. Just for a walk along the shore, or a paddle—oh, and an ice cream.'

'A whippy one with a flake?' Beth asked hopefully.

'Of course. They're the only ones to eat at the seaside,' Lisa said with a grin.

'D'you want to help me make a princess palace?' Beth waved her bucket invitingly.

'A proper sandcastle with turrets and every-thing? Sure,' Lisa said. Then she remembered the last time she'd met Beth. Joel had made it very clear he didn't want her to take up Beth's invi-tation to dinner. Maybe he'd feel the same about the invitation to build a sandcastle, too. Lisa was encroaching on his precious family time. 'As long as it's OK with your dad,' she added quietly.

Joel's glance was unreadable, but he nodded when she glanced at him. 'If you're not too busy.'

Of course she wasn't. She could remember being Beth's age, how important it was to have someone making a really big sandcastle with you—even if they only put a couple of spades' worth of sand in the bucket. If Beth wanted a princess palace, she'd get one. 'What shape's our castle going to be?' she asked.

'Square,' Beth said decisively. 'With a tower at each corner and a big one in the middle. And seaweed on the roof.'

'Don't forget the windows,' Lisa said.

'Windows?' Joel sounded intrigued.

'Uh-huh. Princesses need windows to see out of. So we'll need some shells, too, to make the windows.'

'And a moat,' Beth said. 'Daddy, you can dig the moat while me and Lisa do the castle.'

'Are you sure you've got time for this?' Joel asked Lisa.

'It's my day off. My time's my own,' Lisa said crisply. He might not want to spend time with her off duty, but surely he could put up with her for his daughter's sake? Just for long enough to make the child a sandcastle, at least.

'Thanks.'

He sounded…embarrassed, she thought. As well he should. Her offer had been genuine. And she sincerely hoped he didn't think she was trying to use his daughter to get to him. She'd put him straight on that at the first opportunity out of Beth's earshot.

Twenty-five minutes later, Joel finished digging the moat. Lisa and Beth were patting sand into place and putting the towers in the corners of the castle. They were making a sandcastle together, just like any other family on a beach. The way it should've been with Vanessa, except she'd never really been interested in doing that sort of thing.

Ah, hell. Lisa wasn't his family, and he shouldn't forget it. She was just a colleague. A colleague he found way too attractive for his peace of mind. He should've made some stupid excuse or other, found some reason not to do this with her.

But he hadn't. And she was giving up her free time—the least he could do was be appreciative. 'It's good of you to spare the time,' he said softly, when Beth had moved a few yards away to look for shells to act as windows—still close enough to be safe but far away enough not to be able to hear what he was saying.

Lisa shrugged. 'I like kids. I have a god-daughter who's more or less the same age as Beth. And I know what it's like to lose a parent.' Her voice was equally soft. 'My dad died when I was sixteen. In an RTC—he was driving on ice, and his car wouldn't stop at a junction. He went straight into the path of a lorry. Didn't stand a chance. It was the worst Christmas of my life.'

He sucked in a breath. 'I...' Oh, lord. What did he say now?

She frowned. 'Look, I wasn't gossiping about you, if that's what you're thinking. The reason I know you're a single parent is because someone filled me in so I didn't put my foot in it.'

She didn't say who, but he could hazard a guess. And when—during her first few days in the department. Lisa had just been tactful enough not to say anything to him before now. 'Sorry. That wasn't what I meant at all. I'm just...' He shook his head. 'I don't know.'

She shrugged. 'All I meant was I know exactly where Beth's coming from, because I've been there. I was a lot older than her, I know, but I was still a kid, really, when it happened—still wasn't quite ready to go out into the world. Still needed both my parents there for me.'

'I...' No. 'Sorry' was completely the wrong word. He'd bet she disliked pity as much as he did. 'Must've been rough on you,' he said softly.

'And I can understand now why you don't like driving on ice.'

She shrugged again. 'Something else. Just so you know, I'm doing this for Beth.'

And for the girl Lisa had once been herself?

Her eyes had gone very grey, he noticed. Sad memories, perhaps.

'I apologise.'

'For assuming I was using your daughter to try and hit on you? Good. Because I'm not. And I'm not looking for a relationship with anyone, OK?'

He blew out a breath. 'Whew. You're certainly direct.'

'Easiest way to be. Saves any misconceptions.' She continued putting seaweed onto the curtain walls of the castle.

'OK. I understand that you're doing this because you're a nice woman. And I appreciate the fact that you've made my daughter's day. Thank you.'

She nodded in acknowledgement, but didn't venture any more conversation.

Ah, hell. He didn't want to be at loggerheads with her. He liked her directness, enjoyed talking to her. 'Do you miss London?' he asked.

'I miss my mum—I was just talking to her and trying to persuade her to come up and stay for a few days.'

That 'I love you' he'd overheard had been to her mother?

He suppressed the urge to punch the air. Just.

'I miss some of my friends, too. I definitely miss playing princesses with my goddaughter, Sophie. But I like the fact I get to do air rescues again—in London, it was all or nothing. I'd done my secondment at HEMS, and the rule there is that you're there for six months and then you have to move on.' She lifted a negligent shoulder. 'There's a good reason behind it. Firstly, you don't get over-exposed to trauma and, secondly, a fast rotation means that more emergency department doctors can be trained in pre-hospital care. Didn't give me much of a choice, though. Either I stayed at London City General and couldn't do any air rescue work for who knows how long, or I had to move. So I came here.'

'Why did you choose air rescue?' he asked.

'Because I can make a difference,' she said simply. 'In an air rescue, I can be with a patient within about fifteen minutes of a callout, usually less. They're in the right place for the right treatment well before the golden hour's up. And sometimes I can get to them in the platinum ten minutes.' The first sixty minutes after a medical emergency were known as the golden hour, and the first ten minutes were known as the platinum period—the earlier treatment started, the better the patient's chances were of surviving.

Joel had a feeling Lisa's passion for volunteering was something to do with her father's accident. Probably the same reason that he worked with the coastguard: being able to give something back, and trying to make sure someone else didn't have to go through all that pain and misery.

'Spending your days off at the air ambulance base, you can't have had much chance to see the area,' he said.

'It's only a couple of days a month—not that much, really. And I've done a bit of exploring.'

'Have you been up the coast as far as Bamburgh and Holy Island?' he asked.

She shook her head. 'Not yet.'

'It's a fabulous bit of the coast—Holy Island's gorgeous, though you'll need to check the tide tables before you go.'

'Yeah. Skip was pretty voluble about that.' Skip was the pilot on the air ambulance crew. She rolled her eyes. 'He said they had to rescue a family from the causeway last week who hadn't even bothered looking up the tides.'

'Happens a lot. People just don't think,' Joel said with a grimace. 'And it's worth taking a boat trip out to the Farne Islands, too. In the summer you'll see hundreds of puffins and guillemots. The trips normally land you near Grace Darling's lighthouse—and there you'll get as close to a seal as you are to that sandcastle now.' He gestured to the pile of sand next to her. 'Beth loves it.' He smiled. 'We usually make a day of it—starting with a picnic and ending with a fish supper.'

'Ooh, Daddy, are we having a fish supper tonight?' Beth asked, coming back with a bucketful of shells and overhearing the last bit.

'Not today, kitten. I was talking about when we've been out on a boat to the islands and seen the seals.'

'Ooh, yes. It's brilliant. They're really cute.' She beamed at Lisa. 'You can come with us, if you like, next time we go.' She bounced excitedly on the sand. 'We could go tomorrow.'

'Not tomorrow, honey.' Joel ruffled her hair. 'We have to go see Grandma tomorrow.'

Beth made a face. 'That means I have to be really quiet.'

'Grandma likes seeing you.'

'Can't we go to the islands and see the seals instead?' she asked. 'Please?'

'Some other time,' Joel promised.

'With Lisa?'

'We'll see.'

She sighed. 'That *always* means no.'

He darted a glance at Lisa and, to his surprise, discovered she was laughing.

'What?' he asked.

'Sounds as if your daughter knows you well.'

He waved a dismissive hand. 'All parents say that.'

She smiled wryly. 'Yeah. I remember my mum saying the same thing.'

'Did my mummy say that?' Beth asked.

'Sometimes.' Joel wrapped his arms round her in a bear hug. 'Let's put these windows in the castle, shall we?'

Ten minutes later, the castle was complete.

'Perfect,' Lisa declared. 'Now I need to take a picture of the castle—and its queen.'

'But I haven't got my crown,' Beth said in dismay. 'All my crowns are at home!'

'Ah, but everyone knows that queens and princesses don't wear their crowns on the beach in case they get sand on their diamonds,' Lisa said. 'And you can tell they're a queen or a princess by their smile. You've definitely got the right smile.'

As the little girl beamed, Lisa took a photograph with the camera on her mobile phone. 'There. Lovely.'

'Can you take one with me and Daddy, please?' Beth asked.

'Sure.' Joel was smiling, looking relaxed, and Lisa couldn't resist taking a snap of him on his own, but then she zoomed the camera out again and took the picture of the two of them together.

She bent down and showed Beth, who clapped her hands in delight. 'Oh, it's brilliant!'

'I'll download it onto my computer and print it for you,' Lisa promised. 'And the one of you on your own.' The one of Joel…she'd be sensible, and delete it later. No point in mooning over someone who didn't want her. Someone she couldn't have. Someone who was just plain *wrong* for her.

Beth hugged her. 'Thank you. Thank you so much for helping me, and for taking a picture of me and my daddy.'

'My pleasure, sweetheart.' Lisa hugged her back. 'I'd better let you and your daddy get on now.' The last thing she wanted to do was overstay her welcome with Joel.

'We were going to the café for a sandwich. You're welcome to join us, if you don't have to rush off somewhere,' Joel said, surprising her.

'Please?' Beth asked.

How could she resist? 'Thank you. I'd love to,' she said, scooping up her shoes. 'As long as we have ice creams as well—my treat.'

'Oh, goody! My favourite!' Beth slipped one

hand into Lisa's and the other into Joel's, and skipped along the beach between them.

Lisa's heart missed a beat. This felt like being part of a family again. Except this time she wasn't the little girl skipping next to her parents. She was one of the anchor points.

Which was scary. Really scary. Because it felt right—right enough for her to want to break her no-relationships rule.

But Joel had already made it very clear that wasn't what he wanted. She glanced at him. His expression was completely unreadable. Masked, perhaps. Did this bring back bad memories for him or open the scars again? Ah, hell. That hadn't been what she'd intended at all when she'd agreed to make the sandcastle and have lunch with them.

And right now she didn't have a clue where they'd go from here.

CHAPTER SIX

BEN looked at Lisa, aghast. 'Do you know what you're doing?'

'Looking up a patient's records on Ally's computer.' She rolled her eyes. 'I do know how to work this thing, you know.'

'I don't mean that.' He leaned over and hissed in her ear, 'You're sitting on her chair!'

Lisa shrugged. 'Ally's on a coffee-break. I'm sure she won't mind me using her chair for a few minutes.'

'No, no, no. That's not what I meant. It's *the chair*,' Ben said in a stage whisper. 'The one that makes women pregnant. Do you have any idea what a risk you're running, Lisa?'

She chuckled. 'Ben, that's just superstition.'

'Nuh-uh. Do you know how many people that chair's made pregnant?'

'Coincidence,' she declared. 'I bet whoever took this job was at just the age when she was ready to settle down and start a family.'

Ben wagged his finger at her. 'That's where you're wrong. The one before last—her family was already grown up.'

'Menopause baby?' Lisa guessed. 'They happen. It's a coincidence, Ben. And as I'm not even seeing anyone, just how am I going to make a baby?'

'Don't say I didn't warn you,' Ben said darkly. 'I bet you walk under ladders, too.'

'And I stand on the cracks in the pavement and it doesn't bother me if a black cat crosses my path,' she teased back. 'Relax, Ben. There's really nothing to worry about.' Still smiling, she turned back to the patient's records.

On Sunday afternoon, twenty minutes before Lisa's shift on the air ambulance was due to end, the call came in. 'Tombstoner on the cliffs,' Skip said dryly. 'Let's go.'

'Tombstoner?' Lisa asked, mystified, as they headed for the helicopter.

'Tombstoning's where you jump off a rock or a cliff or harbour into the sea,' Skip explained. 'The higher, the better.'

Lisa frowned. 'That's a bit…well, insane, isn't it?'

'Extreme sport,' Dave said. 'It's popular among the teenagers. They've seen it in ads and magazines and they think it looks cool, so they'll try it. They start on rocks and just move higher and higher. It gives them an adrenalin rush. It drives the coast-guards crazy—they're forever telling kids not to do it and they're campaigning to get notices put up by all the harbours in the area saying that jumping in isn't allowed.' He grimaced. 'It's not that they don't want people to have fun. They want people to enjoy themselves and stay safe at the same time. Tombstoning's just too bloody dangerous.'

'Even if you know the waters well, you might forget about some of the underlying rocks when you can't see them—until it's too late,' Marty added. 'Not to mention being caught by the swell and smashed against the rocks.'

'How do they know the water's deep enough to jump into in the first place?' Lisa asked.

'They don't,' Skip said with a sigh. 'And half of them overestimate how far they can jump out. So they'll end up with anything from a twisted ankle to being paralysed—even dying.'

Lisa assimilated what they'd told her. 'So we're going to rescue a teenager, then?' she guessed.

'No. A thirty-year-old teacher who should've known better at her age. Apparently, she was raising money for the guide dogs.' Dave shook his head in disgust. 'She comes from Cornwall. Says they do it all the time there. But why she couldn't just run a marathon or do a sponsored swim instead…'

'Coastguard's already there, stabilising the casualty,' Skip told them.

Coastguard. The chances were, that meant Joel.

Lisa damped down the flare of awareness and concentrated on what Skip was telling them about the rescue area.

Five minutes later they were hovering above the casualty, as near as they could get to the cliffs.

'Ready to winch down, Lisa?' Dave asked.

She took a deep breath. 'Ready when you are.'

Dave winched her down while Marty kept in contact with the coastguard and relayed directions to Skip.

Arms reached out to steady her after she'd landed on the boat.

Even if her eyes had been closed, she would've known it was Joel. All her nerve-ends were tingling. And she was really, really glad that she was wearing a baggy jump-suit that hid the evidence of her arousal. 'So, what's the situation?' she asked, trying to sound as cool and professional as she could.

'She fell fifty feet off the cliff onto her bottom,' Joel said grimly. 'Query spinal. I've given her analgesia and an anti-emetic and got you IV access.'

'Cheers.' Lisa smiled an acknowledgement at him. 'What's your name, love?' she asked the woman, who was shaking and clearly going into shock.

'Kezia.'

'OK, Kezia. We're going to put you on a stretcher and we're going to put a collar on you that's going to keep your head secure. Don't be scared—it might make you feel a bit hemmed in, but it's only to make absolutely sure that if there is any damage to your spine, we don't make it worse when we move you. Then we're going to lift you up on the winch—I'll be with you all the way up, so don't worry—and then we'll airlift you to the hospital.'

'OK.' Kezia's voice was quavery. Clearly she was trying to be brave, but she was terrified. Terrified that she was badly injured and might never walk again. Terrified that maybe she was going to die.

'We'll look after you,' Lisa said softly, squeezing her hand. 'Try not to worry too much. I can't give you a proper rundown on your condition without seeing some X-rays, but when we get you to the hospital they'll be able to tell you a lot more about what's happened to you and what they can do to treat you.'

Together, she and Joel worked to immobilise Kezia on the stretcher. Lisa snatched a quick glance at him. Something, she thought, was very wrong. Last time they'd done this, he'd chatted to her and to the patient. This time he was silent and she'd never seen him look so grim.

Was it something to do with the tombstoning event? Or was it something else? Was it something *she'd* said or done to upset him?

Then he caught her gaze, and she was shocked by the bleakness in his expression. The greeny-gold in his eyes had vanished, leaving them as grey as fog, and his skin was paler than usual. He looked as if he was in hell.

What she really wanted to do was reach out and hug him, tell him everything was going to be OK. But she held herself back. Apart from the fact she had a patient to airlift to hospital, and time really was of the essence, she knew Joel wouldn't appreciate her drawing attention to him in front of the coastguard team. Especially if he was feeling anywhere near as bad as he looked.

Later. She'd find him later and make him talk to her.

She checked the harness. 'Ready to go,' she said softly. 'Kezia, hang on in there. It might be a bit noisy on the way up, but you're perfectly safe. You're not going to fall or bounce into the cliff or anything like that. We've got you safe and sound. OK, Kezia?'

'Y-yes.' Kezia's teeth were chattering and her breathing was shallow.

Joel quickly checked her pulse. 'Going into shock,' he said economically.

Lisa nodded. 'I'll get her on oxygen and put a space blanket over her in the 'copter. I'll keep an eye on her—if I think she needs it before we get to Resus, I'll start giving her IV fluids.'

'Good plan,' Joel said.

'Ready to go up now,' she told Dave.

She reassured Kezia all the way up to the helicopter and as soon as they were in and had closed the door, she put an oxygen mask on Kezia and a space blanket. She kept checking the woman's vital signs all the way to the hospital. She knew she could concentrate on her patient because Skip and Marty were dealing with the rest of the communications, telling the coastguard and the hospital where they were and their likely arrival time.

A few minutes later they'd landed on the helipad at Northumberland General—and Lisa was relieved when Kezia said she could feel her legs. There was still the possibility of a spinal fracture, but being able to feel her legs again was a good thing.

'I work here,' Lisa told her as she helped push the trolley through to Resus, 'so I'll pop in and see you tomorrow on my lunch-break. Hang on in there. You've got this far and you're not going to stop now.'

Joel really, really hated that particular stretch of the coastline. It had been nearly three years now, but he could still see Vanessa's face. Could still see her poor, battered, bruised face. The lines etched in by misery—so far away from the gentle, smiling woman he'd married. It was an area he avoided as much as possible, and he just hoped that he wouldn't be called out to a rescue at this spot.

But as a volunteer coastguard, he couldn't pick and choose where he went. If he was called to an emergency, he had to put the patient and the team first and his feelings second. So he'd gone out to rescue the tombstoner. Tried not to think about which rock Vanessa had landed on. Tried to function on autopilot.

It had worked. Just. But now he was back in the safety of the harbour, it all washed over him again. Like an undertow, dragging him down.

He couldn't go home yet. Beth would pick up on his misery and it just wouldn't be fair on her. A few minutes more wouldn't make much difference—she was probably playing with Hannah's kids or drawing and having a whale of a time. And a few minutes were all he needed to get himself back under control. Shove the pain back in the little box where it belonged and lock it.

Lisa finally came off her shift, waved goodbye to the lads and drove back towards her cottage. But all the way there she couldn't stop thinking about Joel. About the bleakness in his eyes.

She couldn't just ignore it.

Travelling by boat took much longer than by helicopter. The chances were Joel was still at the harbour. Although she didn't live that far from the harbour, she didn't want to risk missing him, so instead of going home she drove straight to the harbour. Unless she was very much mistaken, the lone figure sitting hunched on the harbour wall was Joel.

She parked the car, then walked quietly over to him and sat next to him. 'Hi.'

'What are you doing here?' he asked, still keeping his gaze trained on the sea.

'Wanted to see you.'

He frowned, but didn't look at her. 'Why?'

'I'm worried about you.'

He shrugged. 'I'm all right.'

'You don't look it.'

That got a reaction. He turned towards her, eyes narrowed. 'How do you mean?'

'Just look in the mirror. You look like hell, Joel. It's not the hospital, I doubt it's Beth or we would've heard about it at work, so it must be something to do with this afternoon.'

'Quite the detective,' he said, his voice dripping acid.

She ignored him: that was obviously the pain talking. 'Is she a friend of yours?'

'Who?' He looked blank.

'Kezia. The woman I just airlifted in.'

He frowned. 'No, I don't know her.'

If it wasn't the accident victim, then it had to be the place. And hadn't Nell said his wife had died in an accident on the cliffs?

'On my first day here,' she said softly, 'I was in a mess and you rescued me—you calmed me down enough to get me down that hill, on the ice. Because you were driving behind me and I knew you were looking out for me, I could put what happened to my dad aside. I could put the fear aside—the fear I'd end up in the same sort of accident, sliding straight into the path of a lorry and being crushed under its wheels—and just *drive*. You helped me. So now let me do the same for you.'

'I don't know what you're talking about.' His face set, he turned away again.

He was obviously hurting. And, whatever he thought, bottling it up wasn't good for him. 'Joel.' She took his hand and squeezed it. 'Sometimes it helps to talk—to someone who's not involved, to someone who's not going to judge you but will just listen. And if you go to pick up your daughter looking like you do right now, you're going to scare the hell out of her. Beth deserves better than that, don't you think?'

He didn't shake her hand free, she noted with relief. But his voice was flat as he asked, 'So what are you saying?'

She took a deep breath. 'I'm saying that I'm going to drive you back to my place and make you a cup of coffee, maybe feed you some cake if I've got some in the cupboard, and you're going to talk to me.'

'Why are you doing this?' he asked.

Because I can't bear seeing you in pain, she thought. Because I want to make it better. 'Because I owe you. That's what friends do— they look out for each other. And we're friends, aren't we?'

He was silent for so long she didn't think he was going to answer her. And then he said, his voice so soft that she could barely hear him over the swish of the waves against the pebbles, 'I guess so.'

'Come on, then. Coffee,' she said, equally softly. She stood up and tugged at his hand. As if it were taking the last of his strength, he got to his feet and let her lead him to her car. He said nothing on the way back to her cottage, and merely nodded when she unlocked her kitchen door and ushered him in, saying, 'Make yourself at home.'

He'd clearly withdrawn into himself again. She didn't push him to talk but simply made the coffee, rummaged in the cupboards to find a packet of chocolate biscuits and set them on a plate in front of him.

'No cake, I'm afraid. This is the best I can do.'

He shrugged as if he didn't care. As if nothing mattered any more.

'So, are you going to tell me?' she asked quietly.

He sighed, and took a draught of the coffee. 'Ugh. It's sweet.'

'And it's probably what you need right now. Talk to me. *Tell* me,' she said.

He put the coffee-mug back on the table and cupped his hands round it. 'It's those bloody cliffs. Vanessa—my wife—died there.'

She waited, knowing that now wasn't the right time to press him—that he needed to tell her in his own time.

Finally, he did. 'It wasn't an accident.' He took a deep breath. 'She jumped.'

Ah, hell. Just like Kezia had jumped off the cliff today. Except Kezia had intended to do it for fundraising. Vanessa clearly hadn't.

'And it was my fault,' he said dully.

She reached over and took his hand. Squeezed it briefly. 'How do you work that one out?'

He took a deep breath. 'She had postnatal depression—very badly—after Beth was born. I didn't notice as much as I should have done. I spent too much time at work and not enough with my family—all because I had this crackpot idea about being on a fast track, making consultant and being able to give them everything.' He closed his eyes. 'Money isn't important. It wouldn't have mattered if Beth wore second-hand clothes or didn't have a houseful of toys. I was too stupid to see that. I concentrated on my career instead of my family—and I lost them.'

'You still have Beth,' Lisa pointed out.

He opened his eyes again and stared at her, his eyes full of pain. 'And I don't deserve her.'

Not true, but she let it pass. Right now, Joel wasn't going to see things logically. He was hurting. And she was sure there was more he wasn't telling her—more he needed to talk about. 'What about your GP? Didn't he notice that Vanessa was depressed? Or the midwife?' For years now midwives had been using the Edinburgh test, a questionnaire all new mums had to fill out to check for any signs of post-natal depression. Even if Vanessa had deliber-ately given the wrong answers—the ones that would make the test result say she was fine—just talking to her should have alerted the GP or midwife that she was having a tough time and needed help.

He nodded. 'Eventually the GP picked it up and sorted it out—but I should've been the one to notice. I might just as well have driven her to the cliffs and pushed her over the edge myself.'

'Don't you think you're being just a bit hard on yourself?' she asked gently.

'I'm a qualified doctor,' he said. 'So I should have noticed that she'd started being withdrawn again. I should have gone to the GP with her, got a referral to a psychologist. She was crying out for help, Lisa, and I wasn't listening. I didn't see the signs. I…' He shuddered. 'I should have *known*.'

'You can't read people's minds, Joel.'

'No.' He dragged in a breath. 'But when someone's had bad postnatal depression, they're scared it's going to happen again. They might put a brave face on for the midwife, but inside they're terrified.' He lifted his head and looked Lisa straight in the eye. 'Vanessa was six months pregnant when she died.'

Lisa couldn't quite take it in. And it must have shown on her face because Joel spelt it out for her. 'She was so desperate, so afraid of having another baby and all that misery starting up again, that she jumped rather than face the future.'

The air felt as if it had been stretched to the point of breaking and imploding. She had no idea what to say.

He'd been carrying this burden alone for two years. A burden of guilt and misery that nobody could lift from him. And her heart ached for him.

'I don't know what to say,' she said honestly. 'I didn't know Vanessa, so I'm not going to insult you by saying I'm sorry. You don't need my pity.' She hated people pitying her, too, when they found out about her dad. She took a deep breath.

'But I do think you're blaming yourself unfairly. Unless she'd given you any idea that was what she was planning, you couldn't have known.'

'I should have *guessed*,' he said stubbornly. 'I should have listened to her. Seen she was getting depressed. Made her tell me her worries.'

'You were her husband, Joel, not her doctor. Her GP, midwife and obstetric consultant all knew her background. They were the ones who should've picked it up, not you.'

He shook his head. 'I lived with her. I knew her better than they did. I should've seen that she wasn't herself, that she was fretting.'

'And if you'd kept on and on at her, wouldn't she have felt stifled? As if you didn't trust her, or were trying to smother her in cotton wool?' Lisa asked. 'Wouldn't that have made her feel worse, if you'd done that?'

Joel went very still. 'Maybe.'

'Maybe,' Lisa said, 'it really *was* an accident. When I'm out of sorts, I go for a walk by the sea. The sound of the waves...it helps me think. Maybe Vanessa was the same, except she liked walking on the cliffs instead of on the shore.

Maybe she was feeling a bit low and needed to feel the wind in her hair and look out at the sea from the clifftop. I can understand that. But I can't imagine anyone wanting to leave a husband she loved and a beautiful little girl like Beth. Scared or not, she wouldn't leave you both. Not deliberately.' Then a seriously nasty thought struck her. 'Was Beth with her when it happened?'

'No. She was at playgroup. That's how I knew something was wrong—they called me at work, said Vanessa hadn't come to pick her up. I had to leave early.' He swallowed. 'I thought maybe she was having a nap, had unplugged the phone so she wouldn't be disturbed but had forgotten to set the alarm or just slept through it. So I took Beth home. And Vanessa wasn't there.' He sucked in a breath. 'Her car was gone. I had no idea where she was.'

'There was no note? No text message or email?'

'Nothing.'

'So it *must* have been an accident, Joel,' she said softly. 'If you're going to kill yourself, you leave a note to explain. So the people you leave behind can understand why you did it.'

'That's what the coroner said.'

But Joel was clearly still blaming himself. 'Joel, you need to forgive yourself. You're only human, like the rest of us. You can't guess what someone's going to do. And you can't stop an accident happening.'

He swallowed hard. 'If I'd been a better husband to her, it wouldn't have happened.'

He really believed that? He really thought he'd let Vanessa down that badly? Unable to stay apart from him any longer, Lisa pushed her chair back, stood behind him and wrapped her arms round his shoulders. Held him close, willing the warmth of her body to ease the pain in his heart. 'Listen to me, Joel Mortimer. I've seen you at the hospital with patients. You're a brilliant doctor. You spend time talking to them, you listen to what they say, and you spot what they *don't* say. And you're the same on the rescue crew.'

He shrugged it off. 'It's my job.'

'But not everyone does it as well as you do. And it's not just your job. I've seen you with Beth, too. You're a fantastic dad. You give her all the love and the time she needs. But you're not perfect.'

He tensed, and she contingued, 'Because it's not possible for *anyone* to be perfect. You're the best dad you know how to be. And my guess is you were the same as a husband. You loved Vanessa, right?'

His breath shuddered. 'Yes.'

'So you weren't perfect, but you were the best husband you knew how to be. And that would've been enough for her, because she knew you were giving her everything you could. It's easy to say in hindsight that you should have done this or said that. But nobody else would have done anything differently, if they'd been you.'

'Wouldn't they?' Tension radiated off him. 'I just feel so bloody guilty. As if I'd stood there on the clifftop and pushed her off.'

'But you didn't, Joel. It was an *accident*. She didn't leave a note.'

'Maybe she forgot. Maybe she was too upset to write one. Maybe she was just panicking so much, all she could think of was ending it. I'll never know.'

She stroked his hair. 'Joel, how many people do you rescue as a coastguard? How many patients do you deal with every day in the emergency department?'

He shook his head. 'I don't know.'

Clearly he was too weary, too miserable to count. 'Lots and lots,' she said. 'The same as I do. And these people don't set out to hurt themselves, do they? They don't start the day thinking, Right, today I'm going to crash my car or get swept out to sea on an inflatable or fall off a ladder. Accidents just *happen*. And you can't spend the rest of your life drowning in guilt for something that wasn't your fault, something that you couldn't have stopped.' She held him closer, pressing her cheek against his. Turned her face very slightly to give him a comforting peck on the cheek.

At the same time Joel turned slightly, too, and his mouth touched hers. Gently, softly, the merest brush of his lips against hers.

And then the fireworks exploded in her head.

CHAPTER SEVEN

JOEL knew he shouldn't be doing this. He didn't have the *right* to do this but, God help him, he couldn't stop. Kissing Lisa was everything he'd dreamt it would be. Her mouth was warm and sweet and responsive. And she was definitely kissing him back, matching him nibble for nibble. When he nipped her lower lip gently between his, her mouth opened and he slid his tongue against hers, exploring the sweetness of her mouth.

His senses were humming. He could smell her sweet, floral scent; hear the blood thrumming in his veins; feel the softness of her skin against his fingertips. This was the first time he'd felt really alive in *years*.

Joel wasn't sure which of them moved, when or how, but then he was aware that Lisa was sitting on his lap, astride him, with her hands tangled in his hair. She was kissing him back, exploring and inciting, and his head was swimming. He couldn't resist sliding his hands underneath the hem of her T-shirt, flattening his palms against her stomach. Her skin was warm and smooth and soft, just as he'd imagined it would be, and he wanted more. Much more. He pushed his hands upwards to cup her breasts; the lace of her bra was the thinnest, flimsiest barrier, and he had to resist the urge to rip it away as she pressed closer to him, shifting on his lap so that her sex was pressed against his.

Oh, lord. He couldn't remember when he'd last felt this turned on. He could feel the heat of her sex through the soft, worn denim and he wanted to sheathe his body in hers, feel her wrapped round him and her soft breasts brushing against his chest and…

Uh. He had to stop, stop this right now. He wasn't free. This wasn't fair to her.

But, oh, he needed to see her. Touch her. Taste her.

* * *

Lisa rocked her pelvis against Joel's. The soft, worn denim of her jeans and the lightweight fabric of his summer suit weren't that much of a barrier, and she was left in no doubt that he wanted her just as much as she wanted him.

Here.

Now.

Oh, please, *now*.

She'd never been so ready in her life.

She was aware that his hands had moved again, that he was pulling at the hem of her T-shirt and moving it, oh, so slowly upwards.

So they'd be skin to skin. At last.

Oh-h-h.

She needed this so badly. Wanted Joel more than she'd ever wanted a man before.

She lifted her arms, letting him pull the T-shirt over her head. As his head dipped and his mouth nuzzled along the lacy edge of her bra, she tipped her head back and dragged in a breath.

Now. *Please*, now. She was going to go crazy if he didn't use his mouth on her in the next second.

His hands slid along her ribcage down to her waist, and she nearly howled in frustration.

And then he let one hand drift up her spine; finally, finally, he unclipped her bra and let it fall, exposing her breasts to him. He nibbled her shoulder as he cupped her breasts, teasing her nipples with his forefinger and thumb.

'Please.' The whisper was dragged from her. 'Oh, please. *Joel.*' She was begging, but breathing was so difficult she couldn't get the words out. 'I...need...'

She felt him smile against her skin, and his mouth drifted down, pausing in the hollows of her collarbone and then, at last, he took one nipple into his mouth and sucked.

'Yes,' she hissed, and slid her fingers into his hair, urging him on.

Oh, lord, this felt even better than she'd expected—better than she'd dreamt. His hair was soft and his mouth was sweet, but it wasn't enough. It wasn't anywhere near enough. If he called a halt now, she'd go insane. She wriggled her pelvis against him, hoping he'd get the hint. And there were definitely too many clothes in the way. Starting with his shirt.

She struggled with the buttons, but finally managed it and pushed the soft cotton from his shoulders. There was a light sprinkling of hair on his chest, and his muscles were well developed from his rescue work. She ran her hands over his shoulders and across his pecs. 'You're gorgeous,' she whispered huskily. Even more beautiful than she'd dreamt. His skin was fair, despite the work he did outside, and such a contrast to his almost-black hair. He'd look truly stunning dressed all in black—no woman would be able to keep her eyes off him.

Eyes? Ha. No woman would be able to keep her *hands* off him. She certainly couldn't. She loved the softness of his skin, the way the hair on his chest tickled her fingers, the hardness of his muscles.

'You're the most beautiful man I've ever seen,' she said.

The sound of her voice made him lift his head. He looked at her, his eyes pure gold with molten desire, and a thrill rippled through her body. He wanted her just as much as she wanted him. He was with her all the way.

'We shouldn't be doing this,' he said softly.

Oh, no. Oh, no, no, no. They couldn't stop—not *now*. 'Yes, we should,' she said firmly. Then she ruined all semblance of self-control by adding, 'If you stop now, I'm going to spontaneously combust.'

'If we don't stop,' he said, his voice cracking, 'I think *I'm* going to spontaneously combust.'

She smiled then and ran the pad of her thumb over his lower lip—his beautiful, sensual lower lip. The mouth that she needed to feel on her body again right now. 'I do hope that's a promise.'

He was very, very still, barely even breathing. 'Are you sure about this?'

She slid off his lap. 'I'm sure.' More sure than she'd been about anything she could remember. 'I want you, Joel. Right here, right now.' She held her hand out to him. 'And I think you need this as much as I do.'

He took her hand, raised it to his mouth and pressed a kiss into her palm, then folded her fingers over it. 'Lisa.' He stood up. 'I find you very, very attractive.'

Yeah. The physical evidence was pretty

obvious. On both sides. Her nipples were tight and there was a definite bulge in his trousers.

'But this isn't…'

She froze. No. Please, no. He couldn't stop now. Could he?

He disentangled his hand and she knew he was going to back away from her. Walk out of her house. That she'd be too embarrassed and ashamed to face him at work tomorrow, remembering the way she'd thrown herself at him and the coolness with which he'd turned her down.

But then he scooped her into his arms, lifting her with one arm under her knees so she had to slide her hands round his neck for balance.

'Oh, yes. That's more like it,' he said in satisfaction.

Her heart missed a beat. So he wasn't rejecting her?

No. He'd just wanted to take control. Be the one carrying her to bed, not with her leading the way.

She could live with that.

He bent his head to kiss her, his mouth coaxing an instant response from her.

'Mmm. Better still,' he whispered when he

broke the kiss. 'But I need to know…where's your room?'

His tone was so urgent, so desperate. She knew just how he was feeling, because it was the same for her. Need. Desire. Simmering through her body and driving her crazy. 'Top of the stairs, turn left.'

He carried her upstairs to her room and closed the curtains, still carrying her in his arms, then shifted slightly to let her slide down his body. The tips of her breasts rubbed against the hair on his chest; the sensation sent a shiver through her.

'Are you all right?' he asked.

'Uh, no. But I think I will be when you get the rest of my clothes off.'

A smile lit his face, softening the intensity of his gaze. 'You're very direct.' Then his smile faded. 'I've told you that before.'

Yeah. When she'd told him she wasn't using his daughter to try and hit on him.

And what was she doing right now? She was naked to the waist, enticing him to her bed, asking him to strip her. If that wasn't hitting on him, then what on earth was?

She resisted the urge to cover herself. Sure, she could push him away out of embarrassment. But that wouldn't help either of them. It would just leave them both empty and unsatisfied and aching.

This was the right thing.

She reached up and stroked his face. 'Joel, stop thinking,' she said quietly. 'We both need this and we need this *now*. I've been going crazy these last few weeks.'

'Me, too,' he admitted. 'I've been having X-rated dreams. About you and me.'

She raised an eyebrow. 'Funny, that. Me, too.'

'Every time your hand touches mine at work, I want to drag you off to my office, close the blind and lock the door, sweep everything off my desk and…' He dipped his head to kiss her. One fingertip skimmed round the waistband of her jeans, then, finally, he undid the top button and slid the zipper downwards.

Lisa's senses went a bit haywire after that. She wasn't sure who undressed who, when or how— but at last they were lying on her bed, skin to skin, the way she wanted it. The way she *needed* it. Joel's clever, capable hands were stroking her and stoking fires in every nerve end; there was an ache between her legs and if he didn't touch her soon she was going to go insane.

'Where?' he whispered, nibbling her lower lip.

'What?' She frowned, completely thrown. What was he talking about?

He raised an eyebrow. 'You said if I don't touch you soon you're going to go insane.'

The blood rushed to her face, burning her skin. 'Oh, no, I don't believe I said that out loud,' she muttered. 'I'm s—'

He silenced her with a kiss. 'Don't apologise. I'm flattered to think I can make a woman like you feel like this.'

'A woman like me?' She didn't quite follow his meaning.

'Clever.' He brushed his mouth against hers. 'Beautiful.' This time his mouth travelled over her jawline. 'And sexy…' he nipped her earlobe '…as hell.'

Oh-h-h.

Exactly what she thought about him.

His mouth tracked down the sensitive cord at the side of her neck and she tipped her head back, offering him her throat. He nuzzled her collarbone. 'Do you have any idea how much you turn me on?' he asked huskily.

No. But she hoped it was as much as he turned *her* on.

'So. Did you want me to touch you here?'

Her body tightened in anticipation. 'Nope. I'd say you're…cold.' Which was very, very far from how she felt. Right now she was sure her temperature was heading towards forty degrees, if not over it already.

Joel nuzzled his way down her body and touched the tip of his tongue to the tip of her nipple. Lisa shuddered and arched towards him.

'Here?' he asked softly.

'Uh. Yes. I mean, no.' She dragged in a breath. 'But you're getting warmer.' And so was she. Oh, lord. She couldn't remember the last time she'd felt this hot.

'Hmm.' He took one nipple into his mouth and caressed the other. The ache between her legs was getting stronger; she needed him now, *now*. She tangled her fingers in his hair and pushed at the top of his head.

She felt him smile against her skin.

'How about here?' He rubbed his cheek against her midriff.

'Warmer.' She dragged in a breath. 'Not. Warm. Enough.' It was becoming increasingly difficult to speak. For all she knew, she was talking complete and utter gibberish.

He circled her navel with the tip of his tongue; in response, her fingers tightened in his hair and she sobbed his name. 'Joel!'

Finally, as if he sensed that she couldn't take any more teasing, he took pity on her and slid his hand between her legs, pressing his fingers lightly against her sex. 'Here?'

'Oh-h-h.' Breath hissed between her teeth. 'Yes. Hot.' Her bones felt as if they were melting. But he still wasn't quite where she wanted him. 'More,' she said hoarsely. 'Please, more.'

He pushed one finger inside her, and she sighed with need. And then his thumb circled her clitoris, stroking and teasing and driving her crazy.

'Beautiful,' he whispered. 'You're so damn beautiful.'

She rocked against his hand, and he shifted

slightly so he could cup her face with his other hand and brushed his lips against hers.

'Better?' he asked softly.

'Yes. Oh, yes. Oh, Joel, *yes*.' Her body was tightening, cresting, and she held onto him as her climax rocked through her.

When the aftershocks were dying away, she realised her face was damp. He brushed the tears away with his thumb. 'Are you all right?' he asked, looking concerned.

'Very all right,' she said. But he'd been so unselfish. Helped her find release while he—well, his self-control must be a hell of a lot better than hers, she thought. 'But, Joel, you didn't, um…'

'It's fine,' he said softly, and gave her a look so tender it made her ache. 'Look, it's been a while for me. I wanted to make sure it was good for you first, because I don't know how good my control's going to be and I didn't want to disappoint you.'

Her heart did a backflip. How on earth could he possibly think he'd disappoint her? She stroked his face. 'Doesn't matter about your control.' She gave a wry smile. 'I've lost mine already. I want you, Joel. I need you.' She moistened her lower lip. 'Inside me,' she whispered. 'Now.'

He gave her a deep, intense look; those beautiful eyes were pure gold with a hot, hungry expression in them. The kind of heat that made her pulse quicken. The kind of expression that made a matching heat rise in her own body and gave her the weirdest sensation that her heart had just flipped over and over and over, even though she knew that was anatomically impossible.

Then he shifted so that he was above her, his weight balanced on his elbows. 'Now?'

'Oh, yes—now.' She slid her hand between them and guided him into her body.

Joel held himself very, very still, letting her body adjust to his.

He'd guessed they'd be good together. But he'd had no idea it would be *this* good. That he'd feel so complete in her arms. That he could lose himself in her and yet know she was with him all the way.

He couldn't remember ever wanting anyone so badly, even Vanessa.

And he really shouldn't be doing this. Lisa had brought him here just to comfort him, to give him coffee and a sympathetic ear.

But when she'd put her arms round him in her kitchen, his control had snapped. Need had taken over. He'd known she would press that soft, kind kiss to his cheek. And he'd moved deliberately so it had landed on his mouth instead.

Just one little kiss. That had been all he'd wanted. He'd thought he'd be satisfied with that.

How wrong could he have been?

In that moment his whole body had turned to flame. He'd needed to touch her, taste her, feel her body wrapped round his—just like it was now. The ultimate in intimacy.

Unable to resist, he stole a kiss. And then another. And another. And then she wrapped her legs round his waist and pulled him deeper.

'Oh, yes,' he whispered into her mouth. He needed this. Needed her. Needed this white-hot spark between them to wipe out everything else.

* * *

It shouldn't be this good, not the first time, Lisa thought. They didn't know each other that well, so they shouldn't be so in tune. It ought to be clumsy and exploratory and a bit awkward and—oh, this was so *good*. The speed and depth of his strokes were absolutely perfect.

Warmth flooded through her. As the ripples of climax began to shimmer through her again, she saw Joel's face change, saw his eyes filled with need and desire, and kissed him hard as they both fell over the edge.

Some time later—she had no idea how much time later—she was aware of her skin cooling. She had no idea where the duvet was, but Joel's body was warm and wrapped around hers, and no way was she going to move.

As if he'd read her thoughts, he dropped a kiss on her hair. 'Lisa. I have to go.'

Real life filtered in sharply. His little girl was waiting for him at Hannah's. This was stolen time. Time they couldn't really have. 'Beth. Of course. You need to pick her up.'

'Lisa, I—'

She pressed her finger to his lips. 'Shh.' Don't

let him say he was sorry about this. She definitely wasn't. Never would be. Whatever happened now, this had been worth it. Those few perfect, stolen moments when they'd been as one. 'There'll be a time for talking. Later.' Just not right now.

He nodded but, to her relief didn't say the words she didn't want to hear. He held her close for a moment—one last snatched, precious moment—then climbed out of her bed and started searching for his clothes.

'I, um, I'd better drive you back to the harbour,' she said, remembering that they'd left his car there.

'It's not that far. I'll walk.'

Because he didn't want to spend time with her?

It must have shown on her face, because he said softly, 'Because I can't trust myself not to grab you again. I could spend hours just kissing you by the sea. And kissing's not going to be anywhere near enough. Especially now I know…'

He didn't need to finish the sentence. She knew exactly what he meant. Same as she felt. She could make love with Joel for hours and hours and hours, and still want more. Because it was absolutely perfect between them.

He pulled on his clothes and bent down to brush a brief, unbearably sweet kiss against her lips. 'We need to talk. Later.'

'Later,' she agreed.

He cupped her jaw for a moment, the pressure of his hand telling her that he didn't want to leave. That he wanted to stay with her. Be with her.

He paused in the doorway, giving her a hot look that sent all her senses haywire and ratcheted her temperature up a few notches.

And then he was gone. She heard the kitchen door close behind him, and she flopped back against the pillows.

This could be the beginning of something really, really special.

Which was a scary thought, but somehow not quite as terrifying as she'd imagined.

CHAPTER EIGHT

'OH, JOEL. That's so sweet. You really didn't need to do that,' Hannah said, but her face was pink with pleasure as she accepted the flowers.

'Yes, I did. I wanted to say thanks for helping me out. Yet again,' Joel told her. 'And because I don't want you to feel I'm taking you for granted.'

'Now, you know I don't think that. It's difficult, doing what you do and being a single parent,' she reassured him. 'So the rescue took a bit longer than you thought, then?'

Guilt flooded through him and he raked a hand through his hair. He didn't want to lie to Hannah, but he could hardly tell her what he'd just been doing. 'Someone tombstoned off the cliffs and it…well, it brought a few things back to me. I wanted to get my head straight before

I came to fetch Beth.' It was the truth—just not the whole truth. Especially as his head *still* wasn't straight.

'Sensible,' Hannah commented.

Yet another thing he liked about his child-minder: she didn't gush with sympathy or pity him. Probably because she had her own difficulties, with her mother's illness, and he'd never given her unwanted advice or made it obvious that he felt sorry for her.

'You all right now?' she asked.

'Yes, thanks.' In a way. Lisa had lightened the burden, made him tell her how he was feeling and made him see how skewed his view had been—that he really wasn't to blame for what had happened to Vanessa.

But he'd just made things a hell of a lot more complicated between himself and Lisa. He'd broken his no-relationships rule. And quite how he was going to sort it out, he didn't know.

'How's your mum doing?' he asked.

'Fine. Until the next time.' Hannah sighed. 'I know she can't help it, but…oh, if only there were some way to make sure she took her medication properly. So that even if she gets a bee in her bonnet about it, she'd still take it.'

'It's tough,' he agreed. Taking medication was one of the big issues with mental health patients—as soon as they started to feel better, they decided they didn't need the medication any more and stopped taking it, then ended up having a crisis and needing closer monitoring again. It was a vicious spiral, and there were no easy solutions. With the medication Hannah's mother was using, she needed regular blood tests to check the chemical levels in case the dose needed adjusting—it couldn't be given as a 'depot' drug that would release slowly in the bloodstream over weeks or even months.

'Daddy, Daddy, Daddy!' Beth ran towards him, arms outstretched. He caught her up and swung her round.

'Hannah said you were rescuing someone on the boat.'

'Yes.'

'Hannah says Lisa rescues people like you do, only she goes up in a helicopter instead of out in a boat.'

'Uh-huh.'

'Did she rescue people today, too?'

'Yes.'

'Wow.' She wriggled in his arms. 'Can I see Lisa's helicopter one day?'

'We'll see,' he prevaricated.

Beth had really taken a shine to Lisa. They'd bumped into each other on the beach or in the village a few times. And Lisa had always spent time chatting to Beth, doing her hair or teaching her a song or helping her make a sandcastle. She'd even—after checking with Joel first—let the little girl try on her lip gloss. A pale, shimmery, summery pink. His daughter had been in raptures, having someone do something girly with her.

And Lisa hadn't laughed at her when Beth had called it 'lip floss'. She'd smiled, clearly charmed by the mispronunciation, then had got the little girl to spell it out phonetically and praised her for being so clever.

Ah, hell. Beth needed a mum. Lisa would be perfect. She had a rapport with the little girl, and Beth already adored her. If he said to Beth that he wanted to marry Lisa and Lisa would be her new mummy, he had a feeling that Beth would be cheering so loudly they'd hear her in Australia.

The problem was, he didn't want Lisa as Beth's mum. He wanted her all for himself.

Especially after what had just happened between them.

But right now there was too much that needed sorting out in his head first.

'It's home and bathtime for you, young lady,' he said, and nuzzled the tip of his nose against hers before setting her back down on her feet. 'Go and say goodbye to Harry and Connor.'

She scampered off to say goodbye to Hannah's children, then came back and hugged Hannah. 'Thank you for giving me my *scrumptious* tea,' she said.

Joel smiled, guessing that she'd learned a new word from Harry or Connor and was going to try it out at every possible opportunity from now on.

'That's all right, pet.' Hannah ruffled her hair. 'See you tomorrow.'

Joel listened to his daughter chattering all the way home, gave her a bath, then read her a bedtime story. She just about made it to the end of the story, then whispered sleepily, 'Night-night, Daddy. I love you.'

'I love you, too. Sweet dreams,' he said, kissing her and tucking her in.

He tidied the house and did the washing-up he hadn't had time to do after breakfast that morning, but he didn't bother cooking himself anything for dinner. Cooking for one felt just that little bit pointless. And he wasn't hungry anyway.

What was he going to do about Lisa?

The problem was, he came as a package. He wasn't going to try on a relationship for size, because it wasn't fair to Beth: if things went wrong, she was the one who had most to lose, the one who'd get hurt. On the other hand, he wasn't in a position to offer commitment. He didn't even know if Lisa *wanted* commitment from him. Didn't really know where he stood.

They'd made love.

And the sex had been fantastic. More than fantastic.

He shifted uncomfortably in his chair. Even thinking about what they'd done aroused him and made him want her all over again. Not good. He'd need a cold shower before bed.

And just because they'd slept together, it didn't necessarily mean she wanted to repeat it. He knew Lisa had turned down several offers of dates, and the grapevine said she was pretty much dedicated to her career. So maybe she wasn't looking for a relationship. Maybe what had happened between them had been a one-off. Maybe…

He had to talk to her tomorrow. Explain that he wasn't in a position to give her anything. And hope that they could somehow salvage a decent working relationship out of this.

The following morning, Joel was on an early shift. He'd slept badly and only a double-strength coffee jolted him awake. He made Beth's packed lunch while she ate her breakfast, got her school things together and dropped her at Hannah's before heading for the hospital.

Lisa wasn't on early shift—he just hoped she was on a late rather than a night, because he needed to see her. Talk to her. Explain. And the longer he had to wait, the more of a mess he knew he'd make of it. Already his stomach felt as if a kitten had been batting a ball of wool through it and tangled everything up inside.

Hell. He just had to focus on his work. His job wasn't the kind where mistakes didn't matter: in emergency medicine, the wrong decision could make the difference between life or death. Right now his patients had to come first. Then his daughter.

And then, way, way, way back, himself.

His chance came to talk to Lisa came just after lunch, when the department was unusually quiet. 'Could I have a quick word in my office, Dr Richardson?' he asked coolly.

'Sure.'

He closed the door behind her and gestured to a chair. And tried as best he could to damp down the urge to sweep everything off his desk, lift her onto it and kiss her until they were both dizzy.

Instead, he walked round to the other side of his desk. He needed a barrier between them. To stop him trying to grab for something he couldn't have.

'Lisa, I don't know how to say this. So just bear with me if I stumble through it.

Yesterday…' No, he wasn't going to tell her it had been a mistake. It hadn't been. He didn't regret what they'd done. But it was something he couldn't repeat. For both their sakes. 'Look, I like you.' A lot. More than liked her. 'But I can't offer you a relationship.'

She said absolutely nothing. Just waited for him to finish.

Well, he'd asked her to bear with him. She was just doing what he'd asked. Only it made things harder, not easier, when she wasn't saying a word. He couldn't read her expression at all. Though he knew he was hurting her because her eyes had turned grey—and he hated himself for it.

He should've been stronger yesterday. Not taken the comfort he'd needed so badly. Not fallen into her bed.

Not fallen in love with her.

Oh, lord. He stiffened as the realisation hit him. He'd sworn never to fall in love again. Never risk hurting someone, letting them down the way he'd let Vanessa down. And what had he done? Fallen in love with Lisa Richardson. A woman who was brave, sweet, kind and no-nonsense. And right now he was hurting her, letting her down.

What a louse he was. A stupid, stupid louse.

He took a deep breath. 'I come as a package. I can't just take a risk and see where a relationship takes me, because I have to consider Beth. It's not fair to her to expect her to share me with someone, get used to them being in her life, and then maybe losing them when things don't work out. She's already lost too much in her life.'

Still silence.

He pressed on, knowing how bad it was going to sound but not knowing how else to say it. 'And marriage isn't an option either.' The mess he'd made of his marriage to Vanessa had proved beyond all doubt that he wasn't cut out to be a husband.

She raised an eyebrow. 'I don't remember asking you for marriage.'

'You didn't.' She hadn't asked him for anything. She'd been utterly unselfish, comforting him with her body when his head had been in a bad place. And she deserved so much better. She deserved someone who could make her happy. Someone who'd make a decent job of being a husband instead of being a failure.

Sir Galahad, she'd called him.

Sir Fake, more like.

'I'm making a total mess of this.' He raked a hand through his hair. 'What I'm trying to say, Lisa, is that most people have a choice: they can try a relationship on for size, or go for total commitment. I can't do that. I can't offer you anything. Between work, Beth and the coastguard, I don't have any space in my life. I'm not going to insult you by suggesting that we have—I dunno, an affair in the evenings when Beth's asleep. That wouldn't be fair to either of you.' And it would feel utterly wrong, making love to his girlfriend when his child was asleep in the bedroom next door.

'It sounds to me as if you're hiding behind your daughter,' she said dryly.

That stung, and he felt his eyes narrow. 'I'm trying to be responsible. She's only five. Her needs come first.'

Had that been what her mother had felt? Lisa wondered. Was Ella on her own now because nobody had ever been able to measure up to Lisa's father—or was it because she'd tried to put the needs of her teenage daughter first, concentrated on being there for Lisa until she'd been ready to fly the nest, and ended up leaving it too late to find a second chance at happiness for herself?

Guilt flooded through her. And anger—anger that Joel was going to make the same decision that Ella had. In years to come, Beth was going to have to live with that knowledge. Chances were, she'd be horrified at the realisation that her father had put his life on hold for her sake.

'What happens when she's fifteen?' Ouch. Too near to her own circumstances. 'When she's twenty-five? Are you planning to stay alone for the rest of your life, Joel?' She dragged in a breath. 'And when Beth's older and she works all this out for herself, how do you think she's going to feel? Is she going to believe that she's stopped you being happy?' Just as she herself had maybe done to her own mother. Maybe Ella had sacrificed herself for *her*, just as Joel was planning to sacrifice himself for Beth.

And, right now, Lisa felt as guilty as hell.

'I *am* happy,' Joel pointed out. 'I love my daughter, I love my job and I love what I do with the coastguard.'

'And what about time for *you*, Joel? What about what *you* want from life?'

He folded his arms. 'I've already told you. I have what I want.'

'Oh, really?' Not from where she was standing, he didn't. He was in denial, and she wanted to shake him into realising the truth. 'What about yesterday? Don't try to tell me you were happy when I saw you sitting on the harbour wall.'

He shrugged. 'Everyone gets bad days.'

Yesterday hadn't been just a bad day. He'd looked as if he'd been standing on the edge of a yawning abyss at the entrance to hell.

But before she could argue any more, he said quietly, 'I don't want to fight. I just can't offer you anything other than friendship. Yesterday… I took advantage of you, and I apologise for that.'

She wrapped her arms round herself. 'You didn't take advantage of me.' She'd been the one to initiate the kiss after all. She'd been the one willing to lead him upstairs, even though in the end he'd carried her to her bed. She'd been the one who'd told him where her bedroom was. The way she remembered it, they'd been there *together*. All the way.

'It shouldn't have happened.'

Uh-huh. She got the message. Joel clearly thought yesterday had been a mistake. And he was the kind of man who didn't repeat his mistakes. Ever. She kept her voice cool. 'So we're just colleagues from now on.'

'I think it would be best.'

She stood up. 'Then, if you'll excuse me, Dr Mortimer, I have patients to see.'

'Of course,' he said coolly.

What had happened to her lover of yesterday? The man who'd been concerned for her pleasure, who'd kissed her and touched her and made her feel as if her bones were melting? Was he really going to let them both walk away from all that promise?

Clearly yes, because he didn't make a move to stop her when she walked out of his office.

He wasn't even going to give them a chance.

* * *

It wasn't until his office door closed behind Lisa that Joel realised he'd been digging his nails into his palms. Four livid red crescents stared up at him from each hand. And they hurt.

But not half as much as his heart did.

His head knew that he'd done the right thing. Better to end it now before they became too entangled in each other's lives.

But his heart was telling him he'd just made the biggest mistake of his entire life—and he was going to regret this.

If you'll excuse me, Dr Mortimer, I have patients to see. So cool and distant. A million miles from the woman who'd sobbed his name as they'd made love. That beautiful, clever woman who'd turned to mush when he'd kissed her, touched her, pushed deep inside her.

He closed his eyes. He really, really had to forget about that. Or he was going to go crazy.

'Larry Johnson, forty-five, acute stomach pains, pyrexial,' Mark told Lisa. 'We just picked him up from the pub. He's been sick in the ambo.'

She could smell the alcohol on Larry, but she

had a feeling this was more than just a case of someone drinking too much. Particularly as Larry was sitting up and leaning forward, rather than lying down.

'Sorry about that,' Larry said. 'Didn't want to be a problem. Been celebrating my promo—' The word ended on a grunt of pain.

'Where's the pain?' Lisa asked.

'Feels like something's boring into my stomach and coming out of my back,' he said. 'It was worse when they got me to lie down.'

'And it's better if you lean forward?' she asked.

'Yeah.' He shivered. 'It was only a few glasses of champagne. Not the cheap stuff either. It's not supposed to do this to you.'

'Has this ever happened before, Mr Johnson?' she asked.

'Call me Larry. No, never. Never known pain like it.' His face went white. 'I'm not having a heart attack, am I?'

She could understand his fear—he was over-weight, probably didn't do a lot of exercise and he was the prime age for a heart attack victim.

'Doesn't sound like it with the sort of pain you're describing, but I'll give you an ECG to check your heart when I've got the pain to calm down a bit and made you a bit more comfortable.' She smiled at Mark as they reached Resus. 'Thanks for your help, Mark.'

'No worries, pet.' He pulled a wry face. 'I'd better go and clean up the ambo.'

'Sorry about that, mate,' Larry said, wincing. 'Uh. I'd offer to do it for you, but—hell, this *hurts*.' He whimpered as a wave of pain hit him.

'Don't worry, I've dealt with worse,' Mark said. 'And at least you weren't swearing at me like most of the drunks do. I'll leave you in our Lisa's capable hands.'

And that was just what she needed, right now: a patient who required her full attention. So she didn't have time to think about the senior registrar who was working only a few feet away. The man who'd rejected her. The man who'd told her he didn't have space in his life for her. At all.

'I'm going to examine you now, Larry,' she said. 'I need you to lie back for me—I know it hurts, but I have to check you out properly. And then I promise I'll give you something for the pain.'

Just as she'd suspected, there was guarding in his upper abdomen, and he was under-breathing to help ease the pain. There was slight abdominal distension, although Larry was overweight and that made it harder to be sure.

'How long have you been feeling like this?' she asked.

'About an hour. Thought it was a bit of indigestion in the pub. I get that now and again. Then it got worse—like it is now.'

Just as she'd half expected.

'OK. I'm going to put an oxygen mask on you now,' she said, 'to make it easier for you to breathe. It might feel a bit weird, but just go with it.'

'All right, pet.'

She fitted the mask, then gave him some pain relief and an anti-emetic. She could see the moment that it kicked in because he sagged back against the bed in relief.

'I'll need to take some blood from you,' she said, 'so I can run some tests. Have you ever had problems with gallstones?'

He shook his head.

'Do you drink a lot?'

He pulled the mask off slightly. 'Depends what you mean by a lot. I don't go out with my mates to get hammered or anything like that. But I have to go out with clients, and if they order wine…well, it's a bit rude not to drink it. I need to keep my clients sweet.'

'And you go out with clients often?'

'Three or four nights a week. And we all go to the pub on a Friday lunchtime when I'm in the office. Look, I don't do anything stupid like drink and drive.'

'Of course not,' she reassured him. 'So tell me what you'd drink, say, on a typical Thursday.'

'Maybe a pint with my lunch, a few glasses of wine with clients at dinner in the evening, a brandy or two after coffee to help me relax.'

The alcohol intake he'd just described was well over the recommended guidelines of four units a day maximum for men. And if that amount of alcohol didn't make him 'hammered', he was clearly a habitual drinker. Her suspicions deepened: it was sounding more and more like pancreatitis. The key to treating it was finding out the cause. Most of the time they could pinpoint the cause as gallstones or alcohol, and her guess in this case would definitely be alcohol, but she needed to be sure there wasn't any other reason behind it.

'Are you taking any medication?'

He shook his head.

'Recreational drugs?'

He grimaced. 'No, pet, that's a mug's game. I'm not that daft.'

'I think you've probably got something called pancreatitis,' she said, gently easing his mask back into place. 'All that means is your pancreas is inflamed. That's the organ that produces the enzymes you need to digest food—and when it's inflamed it sends the enzymes into the wrong place. It's usually caused by gallstones or if you drink a lot of alcohol.'

'I don't drink *that* much, pet. I'm a social drinker.'

Not quite how she would have described it, but she wasn't going to argue right now. 'I'm going to take some blood from you for a few tests, and

I'm also going to do an ultrasound scan to see if I can spot any gallstones forming.' She smiled at him. 'You'll be pleased to know an ultrasound doesn't hurt—it's done by sound waves.'

'Like the thing you use when women are pregnant? I know I've put on some weight, but I'm not *that* fat, pet,' Larry said, moving his mask and flashing her a wry smile.

She laughed. 'If I found a baby in there, believe me, we'd *both* be famous.'

Quickly, she took the blood samples. 'Julie, can you get the lab to sort these for me? I need full blood count, Us and Es, liver function, glucose and ionised calcium, a coag screen and serum amylase, please.'

She was doing fine. Didn't need to ask for Joel's help, didn't need to even *look* at him. As for her body's awareness of him, well, she'd just have to ignore it while she treated her patient. And doing an ultrasound would keep her mind off Joel.

Larry undid his shirt so she could squeeze the radio-conductive gel over his abdomen, but to her dismay the ultrasound showed nothing.

'Need a hand?' Joel asked, pausing by the screen.

Her heart rate sped up. 'Um…' She needed to play this cool. 'If I could perhaps have a word, Dr Mortimer?' She smiled at Larry. 'Excuse me, Larry. Back in a tick.' She withdrew slightly from Larry's bed. Hell, hell, hell. Yes, she needed help—but if only it had been Nell in Resus with her instead of Joel. Even with the sharp scent of hospital disinfectant around them, his clean personal scent was strong in her memory. A scent she could remember on her own sheets.

Get a grip, Lisa Richardson. Put your patient first, she reminded herself mentally.

'Larry has pancreatitis. He's a drinker, and I'm pretty sure that's the cause, but I need to check for gallstones in case it's that as well. But I can't see a thing on the ultrasound.'

'Happens in about fifty per cent of cases,' Joel told her. 'He's overweight, plus there's over-lying bowel gas. You'll need to send him for a contrast CT scan. What's your treatment plan?'

'I'm not sure if this is an acute attack or the first phase of chronic pancreatitis. There's no Cullen sign—' this was a blue-grey colour around the navel '—or Grey-Turner.' Grey-Turner sign was bruising in the groin area.

'Those signs don't appear in every case,' he reminded her, 'and they can take up to forty-eight hours to show. Don't expect to see them straight away.'

'I've sent off bloods,' she said, giving Joel a swift rundown of the tests she'd ordered. 'I'm going to do an ECG as well. But basically I'm going send him up to the ward. Nil by mouth, bedrest and painkillers while we wait for the test results.'

'Good plan,' Joel said approvingly. 'Well done.'

'Just doing my job.' She gave him a tight smile and went back to Larry. 'I can't tell what I need to know from the ultrasound, Larry, so I'm going to book you in for a CT scan—what that does is take a series of pictures of your insides and we'll be able to see from that if you have gallstones. But for the time being I'm going to send you up to the ward. The best thing for you right now is bedrest and painkillers.'

Larry looked aghast. 'But I've just been promoted! I've got to be back at work, pet. I can't just lie around in bed all day.'

'The office will just have to do without you for a little while,' Lisa told him. Just as she would have to do without Joel...except as a colleague. Which wasn't nearly enough. 'It'll be twenty-four to forty-eight hours before we get all your test results back, and then we'll know exactly what's going on. Pancreatitis can cause complications—that's why we need to keep an eye on you.'

Larry's eyes widened. 'What sort of complications?'

'Kidney or breathing problems,' she said. 'But if you do get them, you'll be in the best place to get them sorted.'

'Am I going to die?' Larry asked. 'It felt like it in the pub.'

'Most people make a full recovery,' Lisa said. 'But you need to stop drinking—if you carry on the way you are, you're likely to end up with chronic pancreatitis. That means instead of having one episode of pain, like you did today, you'll get it most of the time, and you might end up needing surgery.'

'Right. No more booze.' Larry looked thoughtful. 'So what happens now?'

'I'll send you up to the ward, and if you want us to call anyone we can sort that out for you. Your bowel needs a rest so you won't be able to eat or drink anything for a couple of days, until the pain and tenderness has settled down a bit— if you eat or drink now, it'll make the pain worse,' Lisa explained. 'But we're not going to let you get dehydrated—you'll have a drip in, so your body will get enough fluids.'

'And then I'll be able to go home?' Larry asked hopefully.

'Once we're happy that it's just a one-off and there aren't any complications.'

Which was how it was between her and Joel. A one-off. No complications…apart from the fact that she'd fallen for him.

Well, she'd just have to *un*fall.

CHAPTER NINE

'WILL you do my hair in princess plaits, Daddy?' Beth asked. 'Please?'

'How about a ponytail instead?' Joel suggested.

Her lower lip wobbled. 'But Lisa did me proper princess plaits, like Emma's mum does.'

He gritted his teeth. Was his daughter *ever* going to stop talking about Lisa?

'Can we go to see her, and she can do my hair?'

'No, we can't,' he said firmly. 'She's busy at work.' Not strictly true, but he could perhaps be forgiven a white lie for this one.

'When she's off duty, then. You could ask her to tea. Or for a sleepover.'

Joel nearly choked. 'She's too old to ask for a sleepover.' And he really, *really*, really didn't want to think about Lisa staying overnight. In his bed. Her warm, soft, naked body nestled against his. Wrapped around his.

Uh. He needed a change of subject. Fast. 'We need to do your new reading book for Miss Robinson.'

'I can't read without princess plaits,' Beth said mutinously.

His jaw tightened and he forced himself not to snap at his daughter. She wasn't being deliberately awkward, she was just a bit tired and out of sorts. It wasn't her fault that he'd made a complete mess of things with Lisa. And he definitely shouldn't take it out on the one person he should be protecting. 'Sorry, kitten, I can't do princess plaits.' Last time he'd tried, he'd ended up putting a knot in her hair that had taken an hour to undo. 'I can do a ponytail and I can do bunches, but that's all. Tell you what, let's do some cutting and sticking instead.' The idea of glitter usually cheered his daughter up.

But not today. Her lower lip wobbled. 'I don't like glitter any more.'

'It sounds as if someone needs a bath with lots

and lots of bubbles,' he said, striving to remain patient with her.

She sniffed. 'I wish Lisa could give me a bath. And she could teach me some songs. And read me a bedtime story. She's ever so good at reading stories. She does all the voices, too.'

Oh, lord. He was really going to lose it in a minute. He'd have to make some excuse to leave the room and go pummel a pillow.

'Honey, it's just the two of us. The way it's been for years,' he reminded her. 'Don't you like that any more?'

Her eyes glittered with unshed tears. 'Ye-es. But…'

'Tell me, honey,' he encouraged softly. 'Tell me so I can make it better.'

Her bottom lip wobbled. 'Sometimes I wish I had a mummy, like everyone else at school. Josh in my class has two mummies, his real mummy and his stepmummy. And it's not fair because I don't even have *one*.'

Joel scooped her into his arms and held her close, resting his cheek against her hair so she wouldn't see the tears he could feel pricking his own eyes. 'I know, kitten. And I'm sorry.' He was trying to be a mother to her as well as a father. Trying so damned hard. But he just wasn't enough. Never would be. So much for telling Beth he could make it better. Not this, he couldn't.

But there was one little thing he could do for his daughter to make her life happier: he could persuade someone to teach him how to do those wretched princess plaits. Several of the nurses in the ED were mums—surely one of them would teach him?

There was one obvious person to ask…but right now, after the way he'd messed things up between them, she was the last person he could approach.

Life, he thought savagely, sometimes really sucked.

It helped that Joel and Lisa were on different shifts for a few days, but he knew he couldn't avoid her for ever. They were on the same team. And, as a senior doctor in the department, he had certain responsibilities towards his juniors. Such as teaching them things. Giving them hands-on experience of more complex cases—like the intubation that was due to arrive in seven minutes.

He found Ben in the corridor on his way to Reception. 'Just the man I was looking for. I've got a case coming into Resus that you'll find interesting and I want to talk it through with you—and Lisa. Can you find her and meet me in Resus in the next couple of minutes?'

'Sure,' Ben said with a smile.

A couple of minutes. He had a couple of minutes to get himself into professional mode. Teaching was something he enjoyed, something he knew he did well. And he wasn't going to let the fact that he'd be teaching Lisa throw him.

A few moments later, Lisa and Ben were standing beside him.

You're a senior registrar giving a house officer and an SHO some on-the-job training, he reminded himself mentally. Don't even *think* about who the SHO is. Focus on the job.

And he definitely wasn't going to give in to his body's urging to pull her into his arms and kiss her until they were both dizzy. Quite apart from the fact they were at work, it was way, way too late for that. He'd already told her it was over.

'Right, today's topic is intubation,' he said, folding his arms. 'What equipment do you need?'

'Pillow, suction, laryngoscope, endotracheal tubes—that is, ET tubes—syringe and clamp for cuff, forceps, tape and lubricating jelly,' Ben said, ticking them off on his fingers.

'Good. You might want to make sure the ET tubes have different diameters and there are some uncut lengths as well as ones cut to approximately the right length,' Joel added. 'And the first thing we do is?'

'Bag and mask the patient,' Lisa said, 'if the spontaneous breathing isn't good enough.'

He was pretty sure she knew the answer, but he asked anyway, 'Why?'

'To make sure the patient's properly oxygenated,' Lisa said.

'Right. Now, a good rule of thumb, when you start an intubation, is to take a deep breath. If your patient isn't intubated successfully by the time you have to breathe again, you need to remove the ET tube and laryngoscope and ventilate the patient with oxygen for a couple of minutes before you try again.'

He smiled at the younger doctor. 'Ben, what can make an intubation difficult?'

'Um, if there's reduced neck movement or a possible cervical spine injury.'

'Any more?' He glanced at Lisa.

Lord, her mouth. He could remember how it had felt against his. How sweet—and how hot. How it had teased his lips. How it had tracked down over his chest, sending his breathing haywire. How it had—

Concentrate. He really had to concentrate.

'Trauma meaning that the mouth can't open easily. Epiglottitis or a problem with the larynx,' Lisa said.

'Good. Another one, Ben?'

'Um…foreign body, vomit or blood blocking the airway?'

'Yup. There's also tracheal narrowing or deviation, facial deformity or swelling, and protruding teeth,' he told them. 'So what can help with a difficult intubation, Ben?'

'Cricoid pressure,' he said

'Which is?'

Ben took a deep breath. 'Press firmly down on the cricoid cartilage with your thumb and forefinger, and support the patient's neck with your other hand.'

'Spot on. So, we have our equipment ready, we've got cricoid pressure. What's next, Lisa?'

'Etomidate and sux,' she said. Etomidate was the induction agent, which helped provide rapid anaesthesia, and suxamethonium was a muscle relaxant to help the doctor insert the tube without damaging the throat. 'When they're effective, you intubate and inflate the cuff.'

Perfect answer. Joel nodded. 'And then?'

'Check the air entry in both sides of the chest,' she said. 'If the tube's correctly positioned, ventilation's good and the cuff's inflated, then you can take the cricoid pressure off.'

'Right. The best way to make sure the tube's positioned properly is to see it pass between the vocal cords. If you accidentally place it in the oesophagus and don't realise it, it's fatal—and sometimes it's hard to tell because breath sounds and chest movements can seem perfectly normal.

If you're in any doubt,' Joel said seriously, 'any doubt at all, just take the tube out, ventilate your patient with a bag and mask and try again. Cricoid pressure—which Ben mentioned earlier—can help here because it pushes the larynx into view. So that's the theory.' He glanced at his watch. 'In about two minutes, you get the practical. Ben, I'd like you to do the cricoid pressure and, Lisa, you do the intubation. Anything either of you want to ask before we start?'

He couldn't avoid looking at her. Her face was perfectly schooled—as his was. They were both on their best professional behaviour. But her eyes were still grey as her gaze met his. He'd hurt her. And nothing was going to put that right.

At that precise moment their patient arrived. He quickly established a history from the paramedics, then nodded to Ben and Lisa. 'OK, team. Over to you.'

They swung into action, and everything was going fine until Lisa asked him to check the ET tube. As he did so, his hand touched hers. Even though they were both wearing gloves, his body went up in flames.

Ah, hell. When was he going to stop reacting like this to her? *When?*

Be professional, he reminded himself. You're teaching her right now. And Ben. You're not going to wreck your working relationship with her the way you wrecked your personal relationship.

'Yes, that's fine,' he said, as coolly as he could.

She checked the air entry on both sides, checked the cuff and the ventilation pressure, then said to Ben, 'Cricoid off.'

'Absolutely textbook. Well done, both of you,' Joel said.

If only life were as uncomplicated as the teamwork in Resus.

The following Tuesday, Lisa was scheduled for a shift with the air ambulance crew. As usual, she was rostered on the Medic One team, along with Skip the pilot and two paramedics, Dave and Julie's boyfriend Marty. Although the shift didn't start officially until eight o'clock, they had to do some preparatory work first. Which was fine by her: right now, she needed to keep herself too busy to think.

She was in the office at half past seven, but the others were already there.

'What do you call this, you slacker?' Marty teased, tapping his watch.

'Caffeine deficiency,' she teased back.

'Here. Just what the doc ordered.' Dave turned round from the worktop and handed her a mug. Just as she liked it, she realised as she took a sip—hot, strong and one sugar. The fact he'd remembered meant they really did consider her part of the team, and that thought warmed her even more than the coffee.

'Cheers. You're a star. Want me to start checking the packs?' she asked.

'Yep. We'll test the equipment, and Skip's already doing the chopper's levels and windows,' Marty told her. It was always routine to clean the windows and check the engine and instrumentation readings, even if it had been done at the end of the last shift.

She checked the contents of the response bags, burns kit and maternity pack, while Marty and Dave checked the monitoring system, ECG and ventilators. Between them, they checked the safety harnesses and splints, then loaded everything into the helicopter.

Once the helicopter was ready, it was time for paperwork. Skip calculated the day's weight and balance, the details from the previous shift were faxed through to headquarters, and then they were able to declare themselves ready to Ambulance Control.

The first call came halfway through the morning. 'RTC, single car with one victim—the driver's been ejected,' Skip told them. 'Let's go.'

Two minutes later they were strapped into their seats; the engine whined and the rotor began to turn, and then they were up in the air. Dave sat next to Skip, taking directions from Control and relaying them to Skip.

'What's the landing site like?' Skip asked.

There was a pause while Dave waited for an answer. 'Either side of the road, it's forest. But we can use the road as a landing surface—the police have put roadblocks up and they're diverting traffic from the area.'

'Good.'

Within five minutes they were above the scene. Ambulance staff were already there, so clearly the patient's injuries were severe enough to need an airlift to hospital. The car was upside down. If the driver hadn't been thrown clear, he probably wouldn't have made it at all, Lisa thought. They'd definitely need a stretcher for this one, plus a spinal board and head collar to immobilise him and minimise the risk of further injuries.

A quick conversation between the police and Dave, and they were ready to make a landing. Dave directed the ground crew to cover their eyes—the downdraught from the helicopter could whip grit and bits of grass or twigs into people's faces—and then talked Skip down. Finally, they landed on the road, and Lisa and Marty climbed out.

'Hey, Lisa,' one of the paramedics called.

She recognised the voice as Mark's—she was on home ground, then. 'Hi, Mark. What's happened?'

'We think his car left the road, hit a tree, rolled a couple of times and threw him out. He's unconscious. Injuries to head, chest, abdomen and pelvis; query spine.' He ran through what the paramedics had done already to stabilise him. 'His GCS is eight.'

A score of eight on the Glasgow coma scale wasn't good. But at least Lisa knew they'd be at the hospital within six minutes of take-off—the quicker they could get the patient intubated, the better. Any patient with a head injury needed anaesthetic before intubation to avoid a rise in the intracranial pressure—not to mention the risks of aspirating vomit. Intubation was particularly difficult in patients with a suspected cervical spine injury, due to the restrictions in neck movement. So if she could just keep him stable on an oxygen mask for the next six minutes, he'd be in a much better place to deal with any complications.

Resus.

With Joel?

No. Stop lusting after someone you can't have and think of your patient, she told herself crossly.

Between them, they got the patient stabilised, slid the spinal board under him, fitted the head collar to secure his head and neck, then transferred him to a stretcher and carried him to the helicopter. Lisa was the last one in and as soon as the doors were shut and the ground crew had moved back, Skip took off.

All the time thinking of ABC—airway maintenance with cervical spine control, breathing and ventilation, and circulation—Lisa rapidly fitted a tight-fitting mask with oxygen to the patient, then put a cannula in his forearm ready for a drip.

'His sats aren't brilliant,' Marty said, checking the monitor.

'I hope to hell that isn't a tension pneumothorax starting. I'd say he's got rib fractures, query sternum.' She checked his pupil response. 'Equal and reactive, thank God. One less thing to worry about. Dave, is the hospital on standby?'

'Yup. Skip told them.'

It was routine for the pilot to tell Control where they were, where and when they expected to arrive, and details of the patient's injuries, but Lisa had been concentrating on her patient and had tuned out everything else.

'Good. And he's coming round,' she said in

relief. The longer a patient was unconscious, the more likely it was that he had a severe head injury. 'Hello, sweetheart. Don't try to move.'

'Where 'm I?' the patient mumbled.

'In a helicopter, on your way to hospital. What's your name, love?'

'Name?'

Ouch. Sounded as if he were confused. 'What do your friends call you?' she asked gently.

'Oh. Brian.'

O'Brien? Or, oh, Brian? Go for the latter, she decided—he'd correct her if she were wrong.

'Can you remember anything that happened, Brian?' she asked.

'No. Head hurts. Everything hurts,' he whispered.

'OK, sweetheart. I'm going to give you something for the pain.' She gave him analgesia and an anti-emetic at the same time, to make sure he didn't end up vomiting.

'About to land,' Dave said, coming round to join them.

Lisa knew that meant they were a few seconds away from the hospital. They'd land on the special area near the emergency department that was kept clear at all times for the air ambulance.

'We're going to lift you up just a little bit,' Lisa explained to Brian, 'so you don't get jolted when we land.' It was standard procedure in cases of suspected spinal injury—any jolts or bumps could make the injury much more severe.

Once they'd landed, they lowered Brian's stretcher back to the floor and opened the doors. By the time they'd lifted him out of the helicopter, there was a trolley waiting to take him to Resus.

Lisa went with them for the handover.

She regretted it when she saw the doctor striding towards them. The person she'd been trying to keep out of her head. The man with the sexiest voice she'd ever heard. The sexiest mouth she'd ever seen. A mouth she remembered tracking its way down—

Oh, for goodness' sake. That was all over, and she had a critical patient to hand over. *Get a grip*, she told herself savagely.

'Dr Mortimer, this is Brian.' She gave him a rundown of the accident as they wheeled the trolley through to Resus. 'Query spinal, possible fractured sternum, ribs, pelvis, unconscious with a GCS of eight when we got there but it's up to eleven now. He's talking but a bit confused. Stabilised at the scene. I've given him morphine and an anti-emetic, he's been on high-flow oxygen but we're not happy with his stats. Oh, and we secured IV access.'

'Thanks. We'll take it from here.' He acknowledged her with a nod—not even a smile, she noticed—and she turned away.

Lord, she hated this coolness between them. But right now she couldn't think of any way to fix it.

Back at base, Lisa and the team went through the routine of replacing kit, checking monitors and equipment, then radioing through to Control that they were ready for a callout.

'Brian's in good hands,' Dave remarked. 'Joel's one of the best.'

'Uh-huh,' Lisa said carefully. The last thing she wanted to do was to talk about Joel. Dave and Marty were both good at picking up what you didn't say, and she really didn't want them to guess what she thought about Joel. Or, worse, guess what had happened between them. Marty would no doubt tell Julie, and then the hospital grapevine would go into overdrive.

'It's good to have him on the coastguard crew, too,' Marty said. 'He always manages to calm everyone down.'

Exactly what he'd done when she'd been stuck on the hill. Something else she'd rather keep from Dave and Marty. They'd tease her for ever about it—unless she explained exactly why she hated driving on ice. And that was definitely out. She'd rather be teased than pitied.

Joel hadn't pitied her. Probably because he knew how it felt to be on the receiving end of too much sympathy.

She wasn't sure whether she was relieved or disappointed when the call came half an hour later and Marty picked it up.

'That was Joel,' he said when he replaced the receiver. 'Letting us know how Brian got on.'

Had Joel maybe hoped to speak to her? That work would bring them back together—

No. Of course not. And she had to stop fantasising. 'So how is Brian?' she asked carefully.

'We were right about the sternum, ribs and fractured pelvis. Add in some pulmonary contusions.'

The high-energy transfer on impact on accidents often caused contusions—grazing or
bruising of the tissues, and as a result blood collected in the alveolar spaces in the lungs and the
patient had difficulty breathing. In severe cases
it could lead to ARDS, or acute respiratory
distress syndrome. It certainly explained the
problem with Brian's oxygen saturation levels.
Although it would show up on X-rays as white
patches, the full extent often didn't show up for
twenty-four to forty-eight hours. Brian was still
in for a rough time. 'Poor guy,' she said.

'He's in ICU for the time being, but he's
stable,' Marty told them.

'Let's hope he isn't going to develop full-
blown ARDS,' Dave said.

To Lisa's relief, the conversation switched to
'terrible medical cases I have known'. And she
could join in and force her thoughts away
from Joel.

CHAPTER TEN

THREE weeks. It had happened three weeks ago. And Joel had made it clear that it had been a mistake, never to be repeated. She really should be getting over this by now, Lisa thought in exasperation.

But she couldn't get Joel out of her head. Couldn't stop thinking about him. Couldn't stop remembering her quiet, intense, focused lover and the way he'd made her feel. The way he'd put her pleasure first. The way he'd kissed her, touched her, teased her. The weight of his body on hers. The feel of his skin. The way his hair had looked gloriously, sexily messy. The heat in his eyes. And that beautiful, beautiful mouth.

This was stupid. So, so stupid. She didn't even *want* a relationship, for goodness' sake!

Liar, a little voice in her head whispered.

OK. So maybe she'd thought about it.

A bit.

A lot.

But Joel had made it clear he wasn't prepared to do the same. Colleagues only, that's what he'd said. There wasn't room for her in his life.

It was just as well their shifts didn't coincide completely, or she'd go insane. At least today she was with the air rescue crew again. And hopefully all their cases would be inland, as far away as possible from the coastguard crew.

'Are you all right, Lisa?' Skip asked when she walked in.

'Yeah, course.' She frowned. 'Why?'

'You look a bit pale,' Skip said.

'You've got rings under your eyes, too.' Marty came over and traced them with the pad of his thumb. 'Actually, you look terrible, pet. Should you be here?'

'Of course I should. I'm *fine*,' she said crossly. 'Stop bugging me. I'm just a bit tired, that's all.' Because she wasn't getting enough sleep. Because she kept thinking about Joel, and remembering, and wishing, and being so impossibly wet about the situation that she despised herself for it.

'You've been burning the candle at both ends. Must be all these young men you keep taking out on the town,' Skip teased.

Ha. She hadn't dated once since she'd been in Northumbria. Maybe it was time she did. The problem was, she had a nasty feeling that she understood where her mother was coming from now. Nobody would match up to Joel. She'd never, ever reacted to anyone the way she'd reacted to him. 'I'm fine. I just need a bit of sleep.' And maybe some vitamin tablets—she'd been a bit off her food, lately, too. Didn't really fancy anything: half the time, when she cooked herself something, it ended up in the bin after the first mouthful.

'Here. A nice strong coffee'll sort you out, pet,' Dave said, handing her a mug.

She took it, but put it down without drinking it. She wasn't in the mood for coffee today. Even the thought of it brought a nasty, salty taste into her mouth, as if she were about to be sick.

Obviously she'd been overdoing things. Maybe she needed a couple of days off. But for now she'd be fine, as long as she kept busy.

To her relief, none of their calls that day were sea-related. No coastguard. No Joel. No reminders of the time they'd rescued the tombstoner. Or what had happened afterwards.

She was still feeling out of sorts at the end of her shift. Premenstrual, maybe. She'd buy some chocolate on the way home—that always helped.

She did a quick count in her head as she walked to her car, then dropped her keys in shock. Her period was *three days late.*

Stop panicking, she told herself. She'd been stressed lately. She knew that stress often messed up a menstrual cycle.

But she'd been stressed before without being late. She could almost set her watch by her period. Every twenty-eight days, even down to the same time of day, give or take an hour.

Her period was late. And she was bone-deep tired. She didn't fancy any of her favourite foods. And, now she thought of it, she hadn't drunk coffee in a week. Hadn't wanted to. And were her breasts feeling just that little bit sore? Was her sense of smell that little bit keener? Had she been to the loo more often than usual this week, or was she just imagining the whole thing?

'Stop it. You're overreacting,' she told herself loudly, retrieved her keys and climbed into her car. 'There's a perfectly reasonable explanation for all this.'

Though there was only one she could think of. She and Joel hadn't used contraception when they'd made love. They hadn't even thought about it, because they'd been so caught up in the moment. And she certainly hadn't thought about it afterwards. She wasn't on the Pill; she didn't sleep around so she didn't even own a pack of condoms; and, with his no-relationships rule, Joel was unlikely to carry one round with him either. If he did carry condoms, then he'd been too carried away that evening to use one.

They'd had unprotected sex.

And she'd sat in Ally's chair.

The chair that had a reputation.

The chair that made people pregnant.

She shook herself. Utterly ridiculous. The

chair thing was just a superstition. A few coincidences: nothing more than that. Their last few receptionists had probably been around the same age and stage in their relationships, that was all. And OK, so she and Joel hadn't used contraception. But the window for making a baby was small. As a doctor, she knew that there was a one in four chance of conceiving if you had unprotected sex at the most fertile time of your cycle. How many couples tried for months and months and months to make a baby without success?

All the same, it niggled at her all the way home. To the point where she drove to the big out-of-town supermarket to buy a pregnancy test—she definitely wasn't going to buy one in the village and have rumours starting. And this would prove once and for all that she wasn't pregnant, she was just *late*. She bought an expensive test, too, an up-to-the-minute digital one.

Two minutes after getting home, she stared at the little white stick.

It was supposed to reassure her. The symbol was flashing so she knew the test stick had absorbed enough urine to get an accurate result.

All she had to do was wait for the two little words to come up. NOT PREGNANT.

How could time move so slowly? How?

The seconds dragged by, like a snail on a go-slow.

She glanced at her watch. Ten seconds? No, surely it had to be more than that.

She stared at the test again. Come on, come on, prove I'm being ridiculous, she urged it silently.

At last, the message appeared.

And it was wrong. Absolutely wrong. It had to be a mistake. Something had to have gone haywire in the test kit. She stared at it in disbelief.

PREGNANT.

Lisa leaned her elbows on her kitchen table and rested her forehead on her clasped hands. What on earth was she going to do?

She was pregnant.

With Joel's child.

Ben had warned her about that chair, and she'd just laughed. Now she wanted to cry.

She was pregnant.

And she was barely on speaking terms with

the father of her baby. He'd made it very, very clear that he didn't want to be involved with her. Which meant she was on her own.

The breath whooshed out of her lungs. She was twenty-eight. Her career was just taking off. She was an SHO, the next step would be promotion to registrar, and maybe she'd become a trauma specialist. Teach others about first-response medicine, air rescue. All those plans she'd made…

And now she was pregnant.

Her career would have to go on hold.

And she'd have to cope. On her own.

What the hell was she going to do?

Eventually, she dragged herself to her feet. Just sitting there wasn't going to help. She needed to go to the sea.

Ha. Just what she'd told Joel that day. *When I'm out of sorts, I go for a walk by the sea. The sound of the waves…it helps me think.*

Maybe it would.

She walked down to the harbour, took her shoes off, rolled up her jeans and walked along the edge of the sea, letting the foam hiss up and over her feet.

Just calm down, she told herself. You're panicking over nothing. OK, so the pregnancy test was positive. But it's not been that long since your obstetrics rotation and you know the stats. Around one in four women have a miscarriage within the first three months; one in a hundred women has more than one miscarriage. It's still really, really early days: the time when a miscarriage is more likely. So you might not even carry this child to term.

She continued pacing. That was one scenario. But the flipside of the statistics meant she had a three in four chance of carrying the baby to term. Probably more than that, given her age: the risks of miscarriage were higher in mothers over the age of thirty-five. She was twenty-eight years old, fit and healthy; she didn't drink that much; and she'd never smoked or done recreational drugs. The odds were stacked in favour of a healthy pregnancy and a full-term baby.

She was going to have a baby.

And that changed everything. She'd always steered clear of relationships, so she wouldn't have to face losing the one she loved. With a baby, she didn't have that choice. She was going to have this relationship, whether she liked it or not. Because this baby was *part* of her.

A termination was out of the question. Even the word made her recoil. Lord, she'd known she was pregnant for less than an hour, and here she was, already fiercely protective of her baby. With that kind of maternal instinct, there was no way she'd be able to consider adoption. She couldn't carry a baby for nine months, feel it kick inside her and respond to her moods and her touch, and then just give it away.

Which meant keeping the baby.

Bringing it up *alone*.

OK, so her mother had been a single parent, Lisa reminded herself—but not until she herself had been sixteen, already more or less grown up. Which was a world away from being a single parent right from the start.

Pacing along the shoreline wasn't helping. She moved away from the edge of the sea and sat on the sand, drawing her knees up to her chin and wrapping her arms round her ankles.

The foetal position.

Ironic, considering what she'd just learned.

But right now she felt way out of her depth. Stunned at the news, at the realisation of how much her life would have to change. And would she be able to love her baby enough? She'd always steered clear of relationships, never let anyone past the line marked 'friend'. Did she even know how to *love* someone properly?

Looked as if she was going to find out.

She sighed. That wasn't the only issue. Because it wasn't just her baby. The father had a right to know. Even though he'd made it clear they were colleagues, and nothing more than that. Joel didn't have room for *her* in his life. Wouldn't have room for a baby in his life. And it wasn't just Joel either: how would Beth feel about all this?

Messy.

Very, very messy.

Lisa knew she could take the coward's way out—she could leave Northumbria, go back to London and bring up her baby without ever telling Joel that he was a father again. But she'd be lying to him, and to her baby. She'd never been a liar, and she wasn't going to start now.

Which meant she had to figure out a way to tell him.

Then she remembered something else: Vanessa had been pregnant when she'd died.

Telling a man that they'd accidentally made a baby would be one thing. Telling a man who was clearly still grieving for the wife and baby he'd lost and blaming himself for their deaths that they'd accidentally made a baby…

Oh, lord. 'Complicated' didn't even begin to describe this.

First off, she'd better make doubly sure. She'd see her GP. Get the pregnancy confirmed.

And then she'd think about how to tell Joel.

CHAPTER ELEVEN

IT TOOK a couple more days after Lisa's visit to the GP for it to sink in. She really *was* pregnant. She was going to have a baby. Someone who was going to depend on her. Someone she'd love automatically, who'd be the centre of her world.

The kind of relationship she'd always chosen to avoid, in case she lost them one day.

Ironic. Because she hadn't chosen this one. It had happened. And although she had a choice— sort of—she knew she didn't want the alternatives. She was going to love this baby.

Though she still had to tell Joel.

The time never seemed right. Over the next two weeks, either work was crazy, or he was about to leave to pick up his daughter, or…

She knew she was making excuses. She just

still hadn't worked out how to tell him. Still hadn't, by the time of her next shift with the air rescue team.

A shift she was confident of taking, because it was still very early days and her baby wasn't at risk. In a month or two she knew she'd have to think seriously about stepping down from the team for a while. For now she wanted to keep life as normal as possible.

'Sea rescue,' Marty said, putting down the phone. 'Lisa, my love, how are your sea-legs?'

'We didn't exactly get sea rescues in London,' she said.

'We do here. So your sea-legs are about to be tested,' Dave said with a grin. 'And we don't have time to give you an anti-emetic, so I guess we'd better bring some bags. Just in case.'

Lisa laughed back. 'No way—I'll be too busy to start noticing the change in the horizon line and get seasick!' The only queasiness she'd felt—well, so far she'd been pretty lucky. She'd only reacted to particularly powerful smells. Which she wouldn't get at sea...she hoped. Because she still wasn't ready to tell anyone about the baby. Not until she'd told Joel. And the way things were going…

She still hadn't found the right time. It was beginning to look as if she'd have to *make* the right time.

Joel's pager went just as he was about to leave the hospital. The sound was shriller than his hospital bleep: with a sigh, he grabbed his mobile phone and called the coastguard team. 'It's Joel.'

'We've had a call from a boat in distress. Two-man crew, the man's in his fifties, having chest pains, and apparently he's the experienced sailor—this is the first time his wife's been out in the boat.'

Chest pains could be anything from a pulled muscle to a heart attack, with a number of life-threatening conditions in between. But they had an added complication here: even if the patient only had a pulled muscle, he wouldn't be able to crew. And they couldn't expect someone with no sailing experience to bring the boat in safely.

'We need you. Stat.'

'Better get the air ambulance on standby in case it's an MI and we need him airlifted to hospital,' Joel said. 'Are you in contact with the boat now?'

'Yes.'

'Ask his wife if they've got some aspirin on board.' Any responsible sailor would have a first-aid kit handy—hopefully it was up to date and full. 'If they have, she can give him a single dose—unless he's been on blood-thinning drugs such as warfarin or he's got a peptic ulcer or he's allergic to aspirin. Get him to chew it carefully—he needs to break it down into a powder so it's more effective. And don't let him drink or eat anything else.' He paused. 'Repeat that back to me.' If his instructions weren't given correctly, it could be potentially fatal for the patient.

The operator repeated it verbatim.

'Brilliant. Talk his wife through it. I'm on my way.'

As he strode to his car, he speed-dialled Hannah's number. 'Hannah, it's Joel. Got a shout to a boat in distress. Hopefully I shouldn't be more than an hour or two late, but…'

'Don't you fret about the little one. I'll give Beth her tea.'

'You,' Joel said, 'are a wonderful woman. Thank you.' He'd pay Hannah for the extra hours of childminding—but he'd buy her flowers, too. She more than deserved them, and he needed her to know he didn't take her for granted.

He'd taken Lisa for granted.

He pushed the thought away. Now wasn't the time. He had a rescue to go to.

The lifeboat crew were soon at the small boat, and Joel went on board.

'Can you patch us through to the boat? I might as well take a medical history while we're on the way and save a bit of time,' he said.

'Hello?' a voice quavered.

'Hello, Margaret. My name's Joel Mortimer, I'm a doctor on the lifeboat, and we'll be with you very soon. Can you answer a few questions for me that'll save some time when we get to you?'

'Yes.'

'That's great. Now, when it did these chest pains start?'

'Just before I called you.'

'You did the right thing,' he reassured her. 'Has your husband had chest pains before?'

'No.'

Not angina—at least, not diagnosed, Joel thought. Which in some ways was a good thing, in others bad, as he'd have a GTN spray handy to deal with the pain if he suffered from angina. 'Is he taking any medication of any kind?'

'No.'

Good—that made life simpler. 'Any allergies?'

'No.'

Even better. 'Any operations?'

'Only…oh, you know.' Her voice dropped. 'We'd, um, finished our family.'

A vasectomy, she meant. Joel smiled to himself. 'That's pretty common. And don't worry, it's not going to complicate things. Is he a diabetic?'

'No.'

'Did he bang his head at all?'

'No. I made him sit down when he got the chest pains.'

'Perfect,' Joel said. 'Can your husband tell me where the pain is?'

There was a pause while Margaret asked her husband the question. 'He says it's in the middle of his chest.'

Central chest: not good. 'Anywhere else?' He was careful not to ask leading questions about pain radiating through the shoulder or arm.

'Just his chest,' Margaret confirmed.

'Can he describe the pain for me? Is it dull, stabbing, or as if something's gripping?'

Another pause. 'Gripping, like a thick elastic band.'

Really not good. It was sounding more and more like an MI.

'Any other symptoms?'

A pause again. 'He said he feels a bit sick and sweaty. And he can't catch his breath properly.'

Really, really, really not good. 'Did you manage to give him an aspirin?' Joel asked. 'And make him chew it properly?'

'Yes.'

'That's good,' Joel said. 'What was he doing when he got the pains?'

'Turning the boat round,' Margaret said.

It could still be a pulled muscle. But Joel's inner

radar didn't think so. 'Did he bump himself against anything while he was turning the boat round?'

'No.'

'Hang on in there, Margaret. You're doing brilliantly. We're almost with you.' He switched back to the coastguard base. 'Sounds more and more like an MI to me. I'll radio through as soon as I've seen him.'

And then they were at the yacht.

'Thank God you're here,' Margaret said, when Joel climbed on board with his kit. Her face looked pinched.

'Don't worry, pet. It'll be fine,' Joel reassured her. He turned to the man sitting on the floor. 'You're Rupert, yes?' he asked.

The man nodded. Joel didn't like the way the man was sitting, with his fist clenched and pressed to the centre of his chest.

'You might have something called angina—chest pain because the muscle of your heart isn't getting enough oxygen. Is the pain the same as it was?' he asked.

'Yes.'

Rest usually relieved angina; this wasn't

looking hopeful. 'I'm going to spray a drug called GTN under your tongue. That may help with the pain, and I need to examine you.' He was pretty sure it was an MI, but he wanted to exclude some of the other possible causes of chest pain first. 'If it's not working or you feel worse or more uncomfortable, just tell me.' He smiled reassuringly at Margaret as he sprayed the glycerin trinitrate under her husband's tongue. 'We'll get Rupert feeling better, and then have him checked over at hospital. I'm going to call the air ambulance because it'll be easier to get him to hospital on a stretcher than it will be to move him on the boat.' Particularly as the wind had got up a bit and the water was starting to get choppy. He gave swift directions to one of his colleagues to call the air ambulance team.

'But…how am I going to get the boat back?' Margaret asked, looking anxious. 'I can't drive it. And if anything happens to it…'

'We'll give you a hand getting in,' Joel said. 'Don't worry. We're going to concentrate on Rupert right now.' Swiftly he evaluated Rupert's ABCs. 'I'm going to give you some oxygen to help you breathe a bit more easily,' he said, fitting a mask onto the older man.

He listened to both lung fields: no signs of a tension pneumothorax or pneumonia, he was relieved to discover. Gently, he palpated Rupert's abdomen, checking for tenderness or any masses that shouldn't have been there: again, nothing. No signs of DVT in the legs and all the pulses were working as they should be, so there was nothing sinister there.

'I'm pretty sure you've had a heart attack—what we call an MI or myocardial infarction,' he said to Rupert.

Rupert pulled the mask away from his face. 'I can't be. I've kept myself fit, I watch what I eat and drink…' He looked horrified. 'Am I going to die?'

'A significant number of people are still alive ten years after a heart attack,' Joel reassured him. A significant number also died in the first three weeks, but he knew his patient didn't need the extra worry of hearing that right now. 'Is the pain easing at all?'

'Not really,' Rupert admitted.

'OK. I'm going to give you some painkillers,

and something to stop you being sick,' Joel said. 'The air ambulance is on its way, and we'll get you to hospital.'

'But we can't just abandon the boat.'

'We won't. And I'll make sure Margaret's at the hospital with you, if I have to drive her back there myself,' Joel promised. 'Don't worry. It's all going to work out fine.'

By the time he'd given Rupert the analgesia and anti-emetic, the helicopter was hovering above them and a slight figure was being winched down with a stretcher.

Lisa.

His heart leapt. He'd known it would be her, of course, but he'd put it to the back of his mind, concentrating on his patient.

'Oh! I wasn't expecting…well…' Margaret said, sounding flummoxed.

'Dr Lisa Richardson,' Lisa said with a smile, proffering her hand. She staggered slightly as the boat rocked, and Joel automatically reached out to steady her, his hands resting on her shoulders and drawing her against him, using his body as an anchor.

The last time he'd held her like this, he…

Need and longing surged through him. Ah, hell. Five weeks of keeping her at a distance hadn't worked at all. He still wanted her. Wanted her so badly. All he had to do was lower his head, brush his mouth against hers, tell her he had been wrong and he was sorry and somehow they'd work it out. For the space of a heartbeat he held her close, and then he straightened up. Close and personal wasn't a good idea. Especially as they had a job to do right now.

'Sorry. I'm not used to boats,' Lisa admitted. 'I normally do this sort of thing on the ground or dangling in mid-air.'

Rupert moved the mask just long enough to say, 'Don't know what you're missing. Messing about on boats is the best thing there is.'

Lisa smiled. 'I'll let you convince me later. I just need a quick word with Dr Mortimer, and then we'll get you strapped in to the stretcher and winch you up.'

So she was still being formal with him? Even here, with the search and rescue team, where everyone was on nickname terms?

And Lisa's, of course, was 'Lara'. As in Croft. Because she was beautiful and gutsy and didn't stand for any nonsense.

He shoved the hurt aside. Apart from the fact that he knew he deserved it, they were here to do a job. Joel withdrew slightly with her and gave her a quick and quiet rundown on Rupert's condition.

'MI, then,' Lisa said grimly. 'Lucky for him they weren't much further out.'

'He could do with an ECG on the way in. Have you got a defib on board?' Joel asked.

She nodded, clearly aware that in cases of myocardial infarction it was best to give an ECG with a defibrillator nearby, in case the patient had another heart attack and his heart needed to be shocked back into a normal rhythm. 'Give me a hand with the stretcher?'

'Sure.'

Between them, they moved Rupert onto the stretcher and strapped him in. Every so often Joel's hands brushed against hers; every time a thrill ran through his body and he cursed himself for being an idiot. An idiot for feeling this way about her in the first place. An idiot for ever letting her go. An idiot for not getting his head straight and working out how to fix things between them.

All the time, Lisa was reassuring Margaret and Rupert about what would happen next and what to expect in the helicopter.

She had a gorgeous voice. Calm and gentle—yet strong at the same time. She was brave and honest and caring. Exactly the kind of person he wanted working by his side.

He stifled the thought, *At home as well as at work*.

'Are you coming with us?' she asked Margaret.

Margaret looked torn. 'I want to—but I can't. I have to bring the boat in.'

'We'll help you, so you're not going to be on your own,' Joel cut in, guessing that Rupert would be worrying about his wife and not wanting his patient to have any extra stress. 'And I'll drive you to the hospital as soon as we get to shore.'

'But…' Margaret began.

'I have to go past there anyway,' Joel said with a smile, 'so I might as well drop you off.' He brushed aside her thanks, and held the stretcher steady while Lisa gave instructions to the rest of her team and clipped her own harness to the winch line.

And then the stretcher was winched up, with Lisa beside it.

All the way back to shore, Joel pretended he was writing up notes, but his heart wasn't in it. The only thing he could think about was Lisa. They worked so well together as a team in a medical situation. What was to say it wouldn't work outside, too?

Though how could he take that risk? In the end, he'd let her down—just as he'd let Vanessa down.

The sooner he got his heart to stop wanting her, the better.

Another week of waiting to find the right moment. Lisa knew she had to do it soon. Really soon. Before she started to show: her skirt had felt slightly tight that morning. Soon people would start to notice. She just had to be brave. Bite the bullet. And tell Joel. Especially as she was going back to London tomorrow.

She *could* leave him a letter. But, no, that wouldn't be fair to dump it on him like that. She owed it to him to tell him face to face.

Near the end of her shift Resus was empty for once and Joel was just removing his gloves.

Now, she thought.

'May I have a quiet word, Dr Mortimer?' she asked quietly.

He frowned at her formality, but nodded. 'My office?'

'Please.'

She followed him to his office, then closed the door behind them.

'So what is it?'

'There's something I need to say.' She took a deep breath. 'You'd better sit down.'

He remained standing, and folded his arms. 'What's the problem?'

She rubbed her jaw, suddenly feeling nervous. She had no idea how he was going to react. Right now, his expression was grim.

It was probably going to be a hell of a lot grimmer in a few moments. Because she knew it was going to bring back some nightmares for him.

But there was no easy way to say this. She had to say it straight.

'I, um…test,' she mumbled.

'Test? What kind of test?' He looked concerned. 'Are you ill?'

'Not exactly.' She looked at him, and blurted out, 'I'm pregnant.'

CHAPTER TWELVE

PREGNANT?

No. He must have misheard her.

But she was still standing there. Just looking at him. It wasn't some sort of joke in poor taste. Joel knew Lisa wouldn't do anything like that; besides, her face was deadly serious.

It felt as if someone had just pushed him into deep, icy water—and shoved his head under for good measure. So shocking that his body couldn't actually process the information he'd just been given.

His office was silent except for the faint hum of his computer and the suddenly loud ticking of his clock. The words slowly seeped into his head, the syllables matching the pace of the clock.

Lisa.

Pregnant.

With his baby.

'How?'

He realised how stupid the question was the moment it left his mouth. She clearly thought so, too, because her mouth quirked for a moment. 'You're a doctor, Joel. You know how these things happen.'

'But we…' His voice faded.

'We didn't use anything,' she confirmed.

No. He'd been too carried away. It hadn't occurred to him at the time—or later. Hadn't even entered his head. He couldn't even remember the last time he'd needed to buy a packet of condoms. Well before Beth's birth, probably.

'And I'm not on the Pill,' she added softly.

Lisa was pregnant.

He couldn't take this in. 'Once.' They'd made love *once*. And they'd somehow managed to make a baby.

She shrugged. 'That's all it takes sometimes. I did a test. Two, actually. And I've seen my GP, who confirmed it.'

This couldn't be happening. It had to be a

peculiarly realistic dream—one of those ones where you were convinced you were at work and then something completely outlandish happened that let you know that you were dreaming after all. If he looked down, he'd be wearing a clown suit instead of a white coat.

He risked a glance.

Nope. It was definitely a white coat.

OK. Then his door would burst open and his next patient would be Frankenstein, asking for the bolt to be taken out of his neck.

Nope. The door remained resolutely shut.

Right, then. He was about to wake up. If he closed his eyes and opened them again, he'd find himself lying in bed…

Nope. He was in his office.

And Lisa was still there.

Pregnant.

He swallowed hard. That was where it had all gone wrong with Vanessa. He couldn't go through this again. Baby, postnatal depression, everything crashing around them in ruins. Especially now Beth was old enough to under-stand what was going on and be hurt by it.

'How long?' The words felt like sand in his mouth.

'Early days. About eight weeks.'

Oh, lord. Lisa was obviously waiting for him to say something. He knew he *ought* to say something. He opened his mouth, but absolutely nothing came out. His mind felt as blank as his voice.

What the hell did he say now?

When Vanessa had told him they were expecting Beth, he'd whooped with joy and whirled her round.

The second time he'd been pleased but worried sick at the same time. With good reason, as it had turned out.

Now… He was lost for words. Lost, full stop.

'I'm only telling you,' she said calmly, 'because I thought you had a right to know and I wasn't going to take the coward's way out and leave without telling you. But you also need to know that I don't expect anything from you—and neither will my baby.'

Before Joel could get his mouth or his body unfrozen, she walked out. Closed the door behind her. And by the time he made it over to the door, she'd vanished.

He swore silently. This was fast becoming an unholy mess. He grabbed the first person he met in the corridor. 'Julie, I need to sort something out,' he said. 'I'll be ten minutes. If anyone needs me urgently, bleep me.' He was officially on duty. He was supposed to be treating patients and be there to give his juniors advice and support when they got stuck. But right now Lisa had to be his priority.

Lisa—and their unborn baby.

And had she just said something about *leaving*?

She'd been on an early shift, so the chances were that she was heading straight home. He walked swiftly out to the car park. No sign of her—and there were so many cars in the staff car park there was no way he'd be able to spot hers and get to it before she did.

Ah, hell. He was two hours into his shift. He couldn't just walk out or get someone to cover for him. He'd have to wait until the end of his shift to deal with this. Though in some respects that was a good thing: it would give him time to work out what on earth he was going to say to her.

And he just hoped she'd listen when he finally found the right words.

To Joel's relief, Hannah was happy to look after Beth for another half-hour after the time he was supposed to pick her up. He knew it wasn't fair on his little girl—that she'd be kept up well beyond her bedtime and she'd be tired in the morning—but he also knew he couldn't leave this until the next day. And it wasn't something he could deal with over the phone either. He needed to see Lisa and discuss it with her. Face to face.

Somehow he got through the day. And at last, at long, long, last, his shift was over. He called in at the hospital shop on the way out—there wasn't time to go to a proper florist's, and nowhere would be open at that time of the evening anyway—and bought the nicest bunch he could find. Then he drove to Lisa's cottage, keeping just the right side of the speed limit. Her car was parked outside and he could see a light on. So far, so good.

Now for the hard bit.

He still hadn't really worked out what to say. Still didn't really know how he felt, if he was honest with himself. Right now, panic was uppermost. But the one thing he did know was that he couldn't let her go through this pregnancy on her own.

He rang the doorbell. Waited. And waited.

He was just at the point of pressing the buzzer again when the door opened.

She looked pale and tired, and her eyes widened when she saw him. 'What are you doing here?'

'Wanted to see you.' Unconsciously, he echoed what she'd said to him on the day of the tombstoning. 'Lisa, we need to talk.'

'I don't think there's anything left to say.' She folded her arms.

'Yes, there is.' He'd already screwed up that morning by saying nothing. He wasn't going to repeat that mistake. 'It's up to you. We can have this conversation here, in your doorway, where anyone passing by and all your neighbours can hear it, or we can have it in private. Your choice. But we're going to have this conversation. It's not optional.'

She stared at him, and for a moment he thought she was going to slam the door in his face. And then her shoulders sagged and she stood aside to let him in.

Walking into her kitchen was hard. More so because the last time they'd been there, she'd been sitting on his lap and kissing him.

But that wasn't why he was there.

And he definitely needed to keep his hands to himself. This wasn't about them. It was about the baby.

'I'll start with an apology.' He offered her the flowers.

'I don't want these, Joel.'

He dropped them on the table. 'Look, I know they're a cheap bunch from the hospital shop and they're really not good enough. But unless I'd gone out to a florist's myself in my break and then had the whole department speculating just who I was buying flowers for—not that I actually managed to get a break today—this was the best I could do.'

She flushed. 'That isn't what I meant.'

Ow. He'd just yelled at her when she was vulnerable and needed him to be kind—needed him to do the honourable thing. And guilt had needled him into being nasty. 'I'm not making a good job of this, but I'm trying to apologise,' he said quietly. 'Because I should have said something this afternoon when you told me about the baby. I shouldn't have let you just walk out like that. I should have made time for you, listened to you properly, talked it over with you.' He raked a hand through his hair. 'You caught me by surprise. I wasn't…expecting your news.' He smiled wryly. 'Pun not intended.'

That smile made Lisa want to cry. Joel was trying to be nice to her.

And she was obviously hormonal because she never, ever wanted to cry her eyes out just because someone was trying to be nice to her.

'So what did you want to say?' she asked, hoping that she sounded cooler and calmer than she felt.

'You might have been left with the impression that I'm not going to accept my responsibilities. I just wanted to reassure you that's not the case.' His gaze held hers. 'Did you say something earlier about leaving? Are you intending to resign your post and leave Northumbria?'

'I…' Eventually, she shook her head. 'I don't

know. I haven't really decided what I'm going to do yet.'

'You don't have to leave.' His face was serious. 'And there's no need to worry about what people are going to say here. Of course I'll marry you.'

She frowned. 'What did you just say?'

'I said, of course I'll marry you,' he repeated patiently.

'No *way*!'

It was his turn to frown. 'Lisa, you're having my baby.'

'Which isn't a good enough reason to get married to you,' she said through gritted teeth.

He scoffed. 'Of course it is. You're my responsibility now. You and the baby.'

The baby, not *our* baby, she noticed. So he thought his *duty* was to marry her? Absolutely not. It wasn't what she wanted—at all. If he'd told her he loved her and he wanted to share their baby, that would be completely different. But no way was she going to be Joel's *responsibility*. She'd been her mother's responsibility and, although Ella had always made Lisa feel wanted and loved and special, Lisa didn't want to be anyone else's responsibility. She wanted Joel to want her for *who* she was, not *what* she was. Because she was Lisa Richardson, not because she happened to be pregnant—pregnant with his child.

'This isn't the nineteen-fifties,' she said crisply. 'People don't have to get married just because they're expecting a baby.'

He rolled his eyes. 'I know that. But it's the sensible option. You're pregnant, Lisa. With my baby.'

Dimly, it registered that he'd never questioned that.

One good thing, she supposed. At least he'd recognised that she didn't sleep around.

'Being a single parent is bloody hard, believe me. You've got nobody to share the worries with. You might have to get up in the middle of the night to a sick child and then you'll be caring for them throughout the day, too, when you're desperate for some sleep—but there's nobody else to take over for just a couple of hours, so you have to keep going. You're the one who makes all the choices. And you just hope to hell they're the right ones, because there's nobody to talk it over with or agree with you or suggest something different.'

He had a point, Lisa thought. Her own mother had gone through something similar. Admittedly, Ella hadn't had to cope with all the broken nights on her own—but it was still pretty tough in the teenage years, when your children were trying to take their first steps towards independence and wouldn't listen to a word you said, insisted on making their own mistakes instead of taking your advice.

But it still wasn't enough to convince her that marriage was a good idea. What had he said about coming as a package? 'What about Beth?' she asked. 'You said you didn't want a casual relationship, that you needed to protect her.'

'This isn't going to be a casual relationship,' he pointed out. 'We're getting married.'

'You said that marriage wasn't an option,' she reminded him. He'd told her straight: he didn't have room for her in his life.

He shrugged. 'At the time, that was true. But the circumstances are different now.'

'How?' she demanded. 'Just *how* are they different?'

'You're pregnant.'

She shook her head. 'That's not the point.'

He raked a hand through his hair. 'Yes, it is. It's the whole bloody point. Look, being a single parent is a struggle. If you marry me, live with me, I'll be able to help you with our baby. You won't be struggling on your own. And Beth likes you. In fact, she never stops talking about you and asking if we can see you. She needs a mother. Your baby—*our* baby,' he emphasised, 'needs a father. So getting married solves all the problems at one stroke.'

Her lip curled. 'Does it?' She didn't want to do what her mum had done: put her whole life into one relationship. To love someone so much that nobody else would do. And then be left empty. And she sure as hell didn't want to be a replacement for Vanessa. A substitute, wanted for what she was, not who she was.

She folded her arms. 'Get this straight, Joel. I'm *not* going to be a substitute for your late wife, the mother you think your daughter needs.

I'm *not* going not marry you. And now I think you should leave.'

'But—'

'No arguments, Joel. I'm too bloody tired for this. I need some sleep.' She knew she was being unfair, probably hormonal, but she couldn't help it. She really needed some sleep. 'And I just want you to leave me alone. Go home. You'll be late picking Beth up. It's not fair on her.'

'Lisa—'

'Just go,' she cut in. She needed him to go, while she still had the strength to stay dry-eyed.

His mouth thinned. 'All right. You've had a long day, you're tired and I need to collect my daughter. But we still need to talk this through properly, Lisa. You're having my baby. *That*,' he emphasised, 'makes all the difference in the world. I'll see you tomorrow.'

'Actually, you won't,' she corrected. 'I'm off duty for a few days now. And I'm going to London to see my mum.'

His expression was unreadable. 'I'll call you tomorrow, then.'

She shook her head. 'I need time. Space.' So she could work things out in her head.

For a moment she thought he was going to argue further. Then he raked a hand through his hair. 'OK. I can understand that. Call me when you get back?'

At her nod, he said, 'Do you have a piece of paper?'

The best she could rustle up was the back of a junk-mail envelope from her recycling box. He took a pen from the inside pocket of his suit jacket and scribbled a number on the back. 'My mobile number,' he said, giving her back the envelope. 'Have a good time in London. Safe journey.'

Stupidly, now she wanted him to ask her to call him and let her know she'd got there safely. But as she'd told him she wanted space and she didn't want to talk to him until she got back...

Ah, she was just pathetic.

So she said nothing. And she watched him close the door behind him before letting the tears fall.

CHAPTER THIRTEEN

Joel lay awake in bed, staring up at the ceiling in the darkness. Three a.m. and he couldn't sleep.

And it had been like this ever since Lisa had dropped her bombshell.

He'd been over and over their conversation in his head. And he still didn't have any answers. He didn't know how long she was going to be in London. When she was going to be back. When she'd call him. *If* she'd call him even. She'd said she wasn't sure what she was planning to do. Supposing she decided to leave for good, go back to London?

No. Absolutely no. He didn't want her to go. He wanted her to stay—to be a family, with him and Beth and their baby. Give them all a chance.

He'd spent the past two days nipping out into

the corridor at work and switching on his mobile phone to check if he'd had a text or a missed call from her. Nothing.

Was he going to get a second chance at being part of a family? Could he make it right this time round? Could he be a good husband to Lisa, a better husband than he'd been to Vanessa?

Four hours later Joel's alarm clock started beeping madly. He still felt groggy from lack of sleep, but he staggered into the shower, turned the water on full blast and freezing cold to wake him up, got Beth up and ready for school, sorted out her packed lunch and dropped her off at her classroom.

'Have a lovely day, kitten. I love you,' he said, hugging her.

'Love you, too, Daddy.'

He watched until she'd gone in the door, then headed for his car. There was something he needed to do that morning before his shift. He stopped off at the florist's for a bunch of pink roses—Vanessa's favourite flowers—then headed for the cemetery. To his relief, nobody was around. He really loathed days when some well-meaning person or other wanted to chat to him and say what a tragedy it was that his wife had died so young, leaving him with a little one, and how they *felt* for him. Did they really think he didn't already know that? And when he came here, he wanted to be on his own. He didn't want to have to be polite.

He took the old flowers from the little pot in front of the gravestone, changed the water, put the new flowers in place, and put the debris in the rubbish bin. Then he returned to the stone, sat on the ground next to it, wrapped his arms round his legs and rested his chin on his knees.

'I have a problem here, Ness,' he said softly. 'I'm not quite sure if I'm doing the right thing. It's been so long since I followed my heart, I'd almost forgotten I still had one.' He sighed. 'I hope you understand that I'm not being disloyal to you or pretending you never happened, because you'll always live on in our daughter and I'm slowly, slowly getting to a place where I can remember the good times and they're out-weighing the bad. I still miss you. But I'm only thirty-two, Ness. I've still got over half my life ahead of me. And our little girl's growing up. She needs someone around who can tell her about girly things, things I don't have a clue about. We both need someone else in our lives. Someone who's going to love us and be there for us—the way you would if you were still here. If I hadn't let you down.' He dragged in a breath. 'And I'm so, so sorry I let you down. That I missed all the signs. That I didn't take better care of you.'

Guilt flooded through him. 'The thing is, I've met someone. Someone I think could be really important to me.' He dragged in a breath. 'More than that. I'm already in love with her. You'd like her, you really would. She's kind and clever and she makes time for people. Every time I look at her, my heart misses a beat. Except…it's a mess. She's pregnant. It wasn't meant to happen. And I'm terrified, Ness. I'm so scared it's all going to go wrong—that I'm going to louse it up, the same way I made a mess of my marriage with you. I'm scared that she's going to be ill, like you were, and I'll lose her as well. And I'm scared that I've already pushed her away so hard she won't want to give me a second chance anyway so it's already too late.'

He knew he wasn't going to get an answer, but saying the words out loud seemed to help.

Though he also knew he was saying them to the wrong person.

'Maybe,' he said softly, 'it's time for me to stop running scared of relationships. Maybe I should just accept that I got it wrong with you, and learn from my mistakes instead of staying away from people as a way of making sure I'm never in a position to repeat them. Maybe Lisa's talking it through with her mum, the way I'm talking to you right now. And maybe she needs to know what I really feel.'

He didn't have Lisa's mobile number so he couldn't call her. Besides, he'd promised to give her space.

But there was something he could do.

He said his goodbyes to Vanessa, then went into the town centre. It took him a while to find what he wanted—a card with a picture of the sea at sunrise and blank inside. Lisa was definitely a sunrise kind of woman, not a sunset. And she loved the sea. He hoped she'd get the message from the picture: a new beginning. But in case there was any doubt… He drove to her cottage, sat in his car and wrote. Poured his heart out. Addressed the envelope to her. Posted it through her letterbox.

And all he could do now was wait until she'd read it. *If* she read it. And, lord, he hoped she would.

London, Lisa thought as she drove back to her cottage, had done her good. A few days of being spoiled rotten by her mother, of days spent walking through beautiful gardens at country houses and just talking.

Especially that last heart-to-heart with her mother.

'Mum…do you ever regret staying on your own?' she'd asked.

Ella had smiled and shaken her head. 'I never met anyone who matched up to your father.'

'Really? Or were you trying to protect me?'

Ella frowned. 'How do you mean?'

'I was sixteen. At that awkward age. Just thinking about going out on proper dates. But if you had been dating a string of men, you wouldn't exactly have been…well, setting me a good example, would you?'

Ella ruffled her daughter's hair. 'There was an element of that, yes. But don't you *dare* start feeling guilty. If I'd met someone who'd made me want to try, then I would've seen him when you weren't around—when you were having a sleepover at a friend's or something. And when I was sure we were right for each other and it was going to work out, I would've introduced him to you. *But*,' she emphasised, 'I never found anyone who made me feel that way. What I had with your father was a once-in-a-lifetime thing, and I just wasn't prepared to settle for second best. We didn't have enough time together, and I'll always regret that he wasn't here with me to watch you grow into the beautiful, clever woman you've become.' Her voice thickened slightly. 'He'd have been as proud of you as I am.'

Lisa swallowed hard. 'You might not be so proud of me now, Mum. I've, um, got something to tell you. I'm…I'm pregnant.' She took a deep breath. 'It wasn't meant to happen.' Even worse, the thought of using contraception hadn't even entered her head—before *or* after. Being a medic, she should have known better. A lot better.

'And the father doesn't want to know?' Ella hugged her. 'Oh, love. You're not on your own. I'm here and I'll love my grandchild every bit as much as I love you. Come back to London. There's plenty of room for you to stay here with me. And even if you decide to get a place of your own I'll expect to be chief babysitter—in fact, if I'm not, there'll be trouble.'

Lisa gave her mother a watery smile. 'It's not that, Mum. Joel says he'll marry me. That I'm his responsibility.'

Ella winced. 'Oh, no. That's definitely not the right reason to get married. If you don't love each other and you don't want to spend the rest of your lives together, then you'll just end up resenting each other and it won't be good for the baby—or for the two of you, for that matter.' She paused. 'Do you love him?'

Lisa was silent for a long, long time. Then she sighed. 'Yes. It wasn't supposed to happen. I wasn't going to fall in love with anyone—I don't want to be like you and love someone so much that the world's only half a place without them.'

'There's a poem I read a long, long time ago,' Ella said softly. '"'Tis better to have loved and lost Than never to have loved at all." There's a lot of truth in that. You can't spend your life avoiding love.'

'You have.'

Ella shook her head. 'I *had* love,' she said. 'And I'm not prepared to settle for anything less. Other people feel differently, want someone else in their life because they don't want to be on their own, and that's fine—I don't have a problem with that and I don't expect other people to do what I've done. I just made the choice that was right for me.' She paused. 'You know, you're going to have to risk it anyway.'

'Risk what?'

'Love,' Ella said simply. 'Even if it takes you a few days to work out that this little being you've brought into the world is really yours, you'll wake up one day and realise that you love this tiny baby. Not the same kind of love you have for your partner maybe, but you'll be prepared to fight dragons with your bare hands for your baby. And, yes, you'll hurt—the first fall, the first cut, the first time someone says something mean and makes your child cry. But you'll be the one who can kiss the tears away. You'll get those special I-love-you smiles, the sparkle in your child's eye, and that's worth all the pain. Don't be scared to love, Lisa. It's worth it.'

'Maybe.'

To her relief, Ella didn't push it. But her next question was a crunch one, too. 'Does Joel love you?'

'I don't know. I do know he's not going to let me close.' Lisa dragged in a breath. 'He's a single parent. His wife died in an accident when she was pregnant. And he's made it clear that he doesn't want another relationship.'

'Because he loved his wife the way I loved your father?'

Lisa spread her hands. 'I don't know. He says he has to put his daughter first. That he can't just try out a relationship and see where it goes.'

Ella stroked Lisa's hair. 'So *that* was why you asked me such a weird question earlier. Because you think Joel's sacrificing himself for his daughter—and you think that's what I did for you. I can tell you now, I didn't, so don't you dare start feeling guilty. Yes, you came into it, but you weren't the only factor in my decision. Not by a long way. You were sixteen, remember. Getting ready to fly the nest. I knew you'd be going to university in a couple of years and leaving me on my own. If I'd wanted someone else in my life, I would've gone looking a long time ago.' She smiled at Lisa. 'So have you met Joel's daughter?'

'Beth? Yes.' Lisa dragged in a breath. 'I like her. I think she likes me. He says she needs a mother and my baby needs a father, so getting married is the sensible thing.'

'It'd be practical, I agree,' Ella said. 'But just because it's practical doesn't mean it's the right thing to do. You're only twenty-eight. Don't settle for being someone's companion. I don't care if Joel is a nice guy—there's no way in hell my daughter is going to marry someone who wants her to fill a role other than being the love of his life.'

'Oh, Mum.' Lisa brushed away a tear. 'Sorry. I'm being wet.'

'Hormones,' Ella said with a grin. 'You wait. A day or so after the baby's born, you're going to be sobbing your eyes out over the most *stupid* little things. The good news is that the hormones settle down again.' Her smile broadened. 'Until you hit the menopause. And then it's like being a teenager having PMT for the first time. Watch out, world.'

Lisa couldn't help laughing. 'Oh, Mum!'

'Whatever happens between you and Joel, I'm here for you,' Ella said softly. 'You're not going to be on your own with your baby, I promise you that. But it sounds to me as if you two need to talk. Be honest with each other about the way you feel. And if he doesn't tell you, ask him. Ask him what he feels about you.'

'Supposing he doesn't love me back?' Lisa asked, her voice cracking.

Ella stroked her hair. 'Then you'll deal with it. You're strong. You'll cope. But don't borrow trouble. Talk to him. *Really* talk—clever as you are, you can't read each other's minds. Be honest. And then things will sort themselves out.'

* * *

I really, really hope my mother's right, Lisa thought as she parked in front of her cottage. I hope things will sort themselves out. And I hope that deep down Joel feels the same way about me as I do about him.

Don't be scared to love, Lisa. It's worth it.

Right now, Lisa wasn't so sure. But she'd trust her mother's wisdom.

She unloaded her car, unpacked the essentials she'd picked up at the supermarket on the way back, put the kettle on and scooped up the pile of post from the mat by the front door. She leafed through it, dropped the circulars in the recycling bin, put the bills and bank statements to one side for filing and paying—and then she saw something that had clearly been hand delivered.

She'd seen Joel's handwriting enough on patients' notes to recognise the neat script on the envelope. He'd written her a letter.

Bile rose in her throat. Why would Joel write her a letter? Was it a 'Dear Jane' one, telling her that he'd come to his senses while she'd been away and wanted her out of his life? That he didn't want to marry her after all? He didn't want her?

She made herself a cup of hot blackcurrant, then sat down and opened the envelope. There was a card inside rather than a letter; she turned it over and looked at the picture. Sunrise over the sea.

Hope.

Was that what was inside the card, too?

She set it down, almost too afraid to open the card. Afraid of what might be there. Whether it would turn the decisions she'd made on their head again.

She took a sip of blackcurrant. There was no point in being a coward. Better hear what he had to say.

Adrenalin pumped through her, making her fingers shake, and she opened the card.

My dear Lisa

I'm not even sure where to start. Except to ask you to bear with me.

Uh-oh. She'd heard that one from him before. Just before he'd told her he wanted her out of his life. Here we go again, she thought. Only it's in writing this time, so the message gets through to stupid little me.

I'm terrified.

What? That was the last thing she'd expected.

I'm terrified for a lot of reasons. I'm scared that I'll let you down in the same way I let Vanessa down. I'm scared that I'll lose you the same way I lost her. But most of all I'm scared that I've already pushed you away because I was too much of a coward to give us a chance.

I understand that you need space. I'm not going to crowd you or push you. But I'm not going to desert you either. We made our baby together, and I'm here when you're ready to talk.

I've already made a mess of things between us. But there's one thing I really need you to know. I don't want you as a substitute for Vanessa. I know you're not her, and I don't want you as Beth's stand-in mother. I want you for *me*.

I love you.

I don't know where or when or how it happened. I think it's been there right from the start, when you were stuck on the ice and you wound your window down just far enough so I could talk to you. The more I worked with you, the more I liked you. I respect you as a doctor. I like the way you are with people.

And that night we made love was the first time I'd felt alive in years. It wasn't a mistake. It was special, and the way you made me feel scared the hell out of me. So I did the wrong thing. I pushed you away.

I want to live with you and love with you and laugh with you. I want to watch our family grow up with you—Beth, our baby, any other children we might be blessed with.

I just hope I haven't left it too late.

Joel.

Lisa blinked hard. Did this really say what she thought it said?

She read it through again. And again, just in case she was hallucinating.

Joel loved her.

He'd written it down. Delivered it by hand. He *meant* it. He wanted to have this baby with her. Wanted to be a family with her.

She crossed her hands on the table, leaned her forehead against them and cried her heart out.

Joel's pager bleeped. He glanced at the display, then headed straight for the reception desk. 'Ally, I've got a shout. Can you sort cover for me, please?'

'Sure.'

'Thanks, pet.' He gave her a brief smile and left the department.

Fishing boat in distress. Sinking. If the crew hadn't been able to keep her afloat, they'd be in trouble. He hoped they were experienced sailors and had lifejackets on—even at top speed it'd take a while for the lifeboat to get out to them, and the longer people were immersed in cold water, the higher the risk of them ending up with hypothermia.

According to the report, there were three of them, so if they hadn't already been separated by the waves they might be able to use the huddle position, pressing the sides of chests and groins and lower bodies together and keeping their arms around each other at waist level to conserve heat. If the boat went down completely, he hoped they had the sense not to try and swim; even if they were strong swimmers, the coldness of the water would drain their strength and they were nearly two miles out of the harbour. Much too far away.

As he walked from his car to the lifeboat station, he rang Hannah. 'There's a shout on— a boat sinking.'

'Call me when you're back. I'll give Beth her tea, if she's still here at teatime,' Hannah reassured him.

'Thanks. I owe you.' Yet again.

He joined the rest of the crew on the boat, and they set off out of the harbour.

'Any update on the details?' he asked Miles, the skipper.

'The distress call was on Channel 16,' Miles told him.

Pretty much what Joel had expected: it was the emergency channel.

'Nobody's seen a flare yet, though,' Miles added.

That wasn't a good sign. 'Anyone else already out there?'

'Yeah—there are four or five other boats in the area and they're on their way to see if they can pick up the crew or bale out the boat.'

'Heard anything else from the boat?'

'No,' Miles said grimly. 'Johnny Masters is the skipper, so that's one good thing—if anyone can get a boat back, he can. Apparently, he took a couple of tourists out on a fishing trip. Control says a squall blew up in the area, so it might have dismasted him and knocked out communications.'

'Yeah.'

But what neither of them said was that even a good, experienced sailor could be caught out if the weather turned nasty.

They pressed on towards the last known position of the boat. And then the helicopter crew called in. 'Flotsam and a diesel slick, over.'

The lifeboat crew swore collectively under their breath. That meant the boat had definitely gone down: bits of it were bobbing around on the surface. They had some co-ordinates to work to now, but the chances of finding and saving the entire crew were sliding down with every second.

By the time they finally reached the wreck site, Joel's mood was grim. They'd had radio confirmation that one of the passengers had been picked up by another boat and airlifted in. Now it was a matter of finding the other two. The squall had blown over as suddenly as it had started, but the survivors of the wreck could have been blown anywhere by the wind and the waves.

The lifeboat was the nearest to the co-ordinates of the wreck. As they neared the area, there was a shout from one of the crew. 'Contact by sight. Arm waving.'

Thank goodness. After all this time in the water, the casualty would definitely have some degree of hypothermia. But at least he was alive.

'Coastguard Nine to Romeo Bravo. Contact by sight. Airlift needed. Over,' Miles radioed through.

The reply crackled back. 'Romeo Bravo to Coastguard Nine. On our way. Over.'

Joel was standing by with his medical kit when the casualty was brought on board.

'Lay him down over here,' he directed the crew. 'It's OK, you're going to be all right,' he reassured the casualty. 'What's your name?'

'Robin.' The man struggled to sit up. 'Where's my brother?'

'We've had someone airlifted to hospital, and the helicopter's on its way back to pick you up,' Joel said, gently pressing him back. 'You've been in the water for a long time so you've got hypothermia.' The human body cooled thirty times faster when immersed in water, and even in the summer the sea temperature rarely got above fifteen degrees Celsius; the longer the immersion, the lower the body's core temperature became. 'We need to get you out of that wet clothing, into something dry, and cover you up.' In cases of hypothermia, you needed to warm the casualty from the inside out. Rewarming too rapidly could lead to warm blood rushing to the heart and causing a heart attack.

'We need to get Johnny out. I tried to stay with the boat. I—'

Robin was gasping for air, so Joel said quietly, 'Try not to talk.' From Robin's pallor, noisy breathing and rapid, weak pulse, Joel knew that the man was going into shock, too. His circulation was shutting down—they needed to manage this quickly or he wasn't even going to make it onto the helicopter.

'Robin, you need to lie flat for me right now. I'm going to raise your legs so your blood flows a bit better to your upper body,' Joel told him, 'and I'm going to give you some oxygen.' With the help of his crewmates he managed to get Robin into dry clothes, covered the back and sides of his head and had a space blanket over him by the time the helicopter arrived.

The transfer was smooth, although Joel was pretty sure that Robin's condition was deteriorating to the point where he'd need admission to intensive care for controlled warming, where they'd be able to withdraw blood from his circulation, warm it and then return it to his body.

'News from the other guy in hospital,' Miles informed the crew grimly. 'He says the boat turned over and went down in fifteen seconds.'

'Fifteen?' Joel stared at him, shocked.

'Johnny went down with the ship, Even if there

was an air bubble in the cabin, it wouldn't have been enough to keep him alive, not for all this time. Search team's going to send a diver down to the wreck.' A muscle tightened in his jaw. 'There's nothing else we can do for him. We're standing down.'

Joel had given Lisa his number before she'd left for London. Scribbled on the back of an envelope. She extracted the torn scrap of paper from her diary and rang the number.

'The mobile phone you are calling may be switched off,' a recording informed her.

Of course. She glanced at her watch. He was probably at work. Although she could call him there, she'd rather not. She wanted to talk to him privately, not in front of the whole department. Instead, she grabbed her own mobile phone and sent him a text. *Home. Got your card. Lisa.*

And when he got her message…he'd ring her. She hoped.

* * *

By the time the lifeboat crew were back in the harbour, the message was waiting for them. The divers had recovered a body from the boat. Johnny Masters. He hadn't had a chance of getting out.

The mood among the coastguard team was sombre. Everyone had known and liked Johnny; he'd been a fisherman in the area for nearly forty years. What he hadn't known about the sea wasn't worth knowing. He'd been one of the volunteer coastguards, too—when he hadn't been out fishing, he'd been the first to call in on a shout. He'd taught Joel a lot of what he knew now. And even the most hard-boiled among the village teenagers had respected Johnny and hadn't cheeked him—they had been more likely to beg him for a fishing trip.

His family were going to be devastated.

And it was the first fatality the coastguard team had had since Vanessa.

Ah, hell, Joel thought.

The village was going to be just as upset this time. One of their own had been taken by the sea. Last time Joel had shut off and vowed he'd never let himself go through this pain again. Now… Now he knew there were other ways of dealing with it. Better ways.

Soberly he took his mobile phone from his pocket and rang Hannah. 'It's me. It was Johnny Masters.' He took a deep breath. 'Bad news, I'm afraid. He went down with his boat.'

'Oh, no. Poor Valerie. Does she…?'

'Yeah. The police have broken the news,' he said quietly.

There was a loud beep in his ear: an incoming text message, Joel realised. He'd deal with it later.

'I'll hang onto Beth for a bit longer,' Hannah said, her voice slightly shaky. 'You'll need some time. He's the first since—' She broke off.

'The first since Vanessa. Yeah.' He sighed. 'I'm sorry to ring you with bad news. I'll see you soon.'

When he'd ended the call he flicked into the text screen. Missed call: private number. Well, whoever it was would ring him back if it was that urgent.

His phone beeped again; he didn't recognise the number. Frowning slightly, he flicked into the message.

Home. Got your card. Lisa.

It didn't say anything about 'leave me alone' or 'too late' or…

His breath shuddered. Please, let there be hope.

He'd already waited too long; he didn't want to wait any more. After checking there was nothing else he needed to do for the coastguard, he drove to Lisa's cottage. Parked. Rang the doorbell. Waited.

What was she doing, letting a snail lead the way?

'C'mon, c'mon,' he muttered, drumming his fingers against his thigh.

Finally, she opened the door.

'Welcome home,' he said softly. 'I got your text. Do I assume you're ready to talk to me?'

She smiled. 'Yes. I'm ready.'

CHAPTER FOURTEEN

'COME and sit down.' Lisa ushered Joel into the living room. But he noticed that she chose to sit in a chair furthest from him rather than next to him on the sofa.

Putting distance between them.

What he really wanted to do was scoop her up, settle her on his lap and hold her close, just close his eyes and breathe in her scent until he was calm again. Rest his hand over her abdomen, cradle the little life they'd made between them.

But he knew that if he rushed her now, he'd blow it. And this was too important to wreck through impatience.

So he'd take it slowly. Be nice. Polite. As if they were strangers, not lovers. Until he could find the way through to her heart. 'How was London?' he asked.

'Good. How's Beth?'

'Fine. She's with Hannah right now.'

'Is everything all right at the hospital?' she asked.

He shrugged. 'No idea.'

She looked surprised. 'Weren't you on duty today?'

'Yes, but I was called on a shout. The air crew were out, too.'

She frowned. 'What happened?'

'A boat sank in a squall. Two of the sailors are in hospital with hypothermia.' He paused, debating about whether he should tell her, then decided honesty was best. She'd find out soon enough: it would be better coming from him. 'The skipper didn't make it.'

She winced. 'I really hate that kind of shout— where you're racing to get there in time to make everything all right, and it's too late. Was it anyone you knew?'

He nodded. 'Johnny Masters.'

Her eyes widened. 'Johnny whose wife Valerie runs the fish stall on the Friday market?'

'Yup.' So she knew him, too. Not surprising, really. 'Johnny taught me to swim when I was a kid.' Joel, and most of the rest of the kids in the village. He'd drummed it into them about water safety, about paying attention to warning flags and keeping dinghies on a fixed line, not drifting out to sea on an inflatable and getting stuck. 'He taught me my lifeguard skills, too. And worked on the lifeboat crew when he wasn't out fishing. I've known him since I was ten, when my parents first moved here. If anyone could've survived, it would've been him. He knew the sea inside out. But the boat went down in fifteen seconds. He didn't stand a chance.'

She blew out a breath. 'That's… Oh, hell. You must be feeling horrible right now.'

'Yup.' He laced his fingers together. Horrible didn't even begin to describe it. He'd known and liked and respected Johnny—and he'd never see him again. Never talk to him about the sea and fishing and boats and rescue techniques. The loss would leave a hole in his life.

But this time he was going to deal with the loss differently. Not withdraw into himself, the way he had when Vanessa had died. 'The whole crew's pretty much in the doldrums. It's the first fatality since…' Say it. Say her name, he told himself fiercely. 'Since Vanessa's accident. And when the news gets round the village, just about everyone's going to feel bad about it. Everyone knew Johnny. Everyone liked him.' He shook himself. 'But this isn't about me. How are *you* feeling?'

'OK, but a bit tired,' she admitted. 'And before you ask, yes, I took proper breaks from driving on my way back from London. Actually, I was asleep on the sofa when you rang the doorbell.'

No wonder she'd taken ages to answer. And, right now, probably feeling the bone-deep tiredness of early pregnancy, she needed all she sleep she could get. 'Sorry,' he said softly. Maybe he should have phoned her instead. Texted her. Agreed to meet her at a time and place of her choosing.

She shrugged. 'No matter. I wanted to talk to you anyway. I, um, read your card.'

And he didn't have a clue what she thought about it. Her voice and her expression were carefully neutral. Did she want to be with him? Or did she want him to leave her alone and stay out of her life—and the baby's?

He didn't have a clue.

Silence stretched between them. On and on and on. It looked as if he was going to have to be the one who broke it. 'And?' he asked softly.

'Did you mean it?'

That slight breathlessness gave him a clue. She wanted to hear him say it. She wanted him to tell her the truth. Tell her how he felt. OK. He could do that. 'Yes. And you were absolutely right. I was hiding behind my daughter because I was scared.' He smiled thinly. 'At work, I deal with life and death every day. I'm not scared there. Not because I'm arrogant and think I know everything—because I'm confident.'

'There's a difference,' she agreed.

'I've done this job for years. I know what I'm doing and I listen to my patients. Though I also know my limits. If I'm not sure which treatment would be the right one in a particular case, I'll call on a specialist in that area. If I miss something—the bottom line is, I'm part of a team. Someone else is going to notice what I missed and tell me so. And I listen to my team, I don't brush people aside. But when it comes to relationships…it's a completely different ballgame. One where I don't have the right skills.' He closed his eyes briefly. He still didn't have the right skills. Look how he'd messed things up with Lisa, the day after they'd made love. Look how he was fumbling now. 'I've failed badly in my personal life—and my mistakes cost my wife her life and my daughter her mother.'

'What happened to Vanessa was an accident, Joel.'

'Maybe, maybe not.' He shook his head. 'I don't think I'll ever really know the truth. But I could've stopped it happening if I'd taken more notice. If I'd read the signs. If I hadn't got wrapped up in things that weren't as important as I thought they were. And it was the fact I'd messed up so badly that scared me. Stopped me wanting to try again. It made me think: if I got involved with someone else, supposing I made the same mistakes? All the hurt and the pain—it wouldn't be just mine any more. It would be my daughter's as well, because I come as a package.

And it's not fair to make Beth pay for my mistakes again. She's already paid too dearly, much too young.' He took a deep breath. 'So I kept myself shut off. I don't go out on team nights out because babysitting's a problem—but if I was really that determined to go, I could find a way around it, just as I do when I'm out on a shout. I just never wanted to. It was easier to keep everyone at that little bit of a distance. Having a decent working relationship with people but not letting anybody any closer.' He paused. 'Until you.'

'Until me.'

'There was just something about you. I dunno. I brush against people all the time at work and never even notice—when I hand someone a file or an X-ray film or a blood sample or a piece of equipment. But whenever it was you… Even if I was wearing gloves, I was just so aware of the warmth of your skin against mine. And it sent me up in flames. That scared me, too,' he admitted. 'You got past my barriers. My self-control was getting thinner and thinner. I just wanted to grab you and carry you to bed.' Pretty much what he'd actually done, in the end. 'It wasn't just lust either. I find you attractive.' He smiled ruefully. 'I think you already know that. But I like who you are, too. I like it that you have time for people—that you'll spend time reassuring patients and their relatives, you'll spent time teaching junior staff, and you don't do it as if it's a chore.' He smiled at one particular memory. 'That you'll spend precious time off making sandcastles with a little girl, and braiding her hair because her hopeless father still hasn't got the hang of plaits.'

Her face shuttered. 'So you're still looking at me as a substitute.'

He shook his head. 'Definitely not. You're not Vanessa, and I don't want to try to make you into her. I don't want to change anything about you, Lisa. You're direct and you're honest, and I like you that way. And maybe it's time I was direct and honest with you, too.'

'How do you mean?'

'About Vanessa. I loved her deeply,' Joel said quietly. 'And I'm not going to forget her or pretend she never existed. I see her in Beth every day. She'll always be part of my life.' He remembered the words he'd flung at Lisa to push her away. *There's no room for you in my life.* How wrong he'd been. 'There's room in my life for you and our baby, too,' he said softly. 'If you want to be there.'

And how he wanted them there.

'When my mum lost my dad,' Lisa said slowly, 'it was the end of the world for her. Her whole life stopped. She never wanted to find anyone else because nobody would ever match up to him. And I didn't want that to happen to me. I didn't want to love someone so much that without them there's nothing left.' She dragged in a breath. 'And I'm scared, too—scared I won't love my baby enough. Scared I'll make a rubbish mum.'

He smiled. 'If you're worrying about that, it means you'll be a brilliant mum. And I seem to remember someone once telling me that I didn't have to be perfect—I just had to be the best I could be, and that would be enough.'

'Yeah.' She smiled wryly.

'As for the other bit—about life stopping when you lose the one you love—it doesn't always work that way,' he said. 'Life doesn't stop. It moves on, and eventually you move with it. When you want to. When you're ready. When you meet the person who makes you want to move on. You've taught me that.' He looked at her. 'I'm never going to forget Vanessa, but I'm ready to move on. Lisa, I want to share my life with you. I want to make a family with you.'

She still didn't look particularly convinced. He knew he was going to have to take the risk. Say it out loud. 'I love you. I want to marry you.'

She bit her lip. 'But what about Beth? As you said, you come as a package. You need to consider her feelings, too.'

'She's been giving me quite a bit of grief about when she's going to see you again,' Joel said dryly. 'She likes you.'

'That isn't the same as wanting me in her life full time and having to share you with me. And what about the baby? How's she going to feel about that?'

'I don't know,' he said honestly. 'But what I do know is that we can work it out—together. I've learned where I/went wrong in the past. I can't promise I won't still make mistakes in the future, but I'm going to be the best husband and father I can. If you'll let me. And if...' How could such a little word have such a big impact on his life? 'If you want me.'

'You want me for myself? This isn't just because I'm pregnant and because Beth needs a mother-figure in her life?'

'I want you for *you*,' Joel confirmed. 'Because my heart beats faster every time I look at you. Because even if it's bucketing down with rain, when you smile it feels as if the sun's shining. Because I like the way your mind works. Because you're brave enough to winch out of a helicopter to rescue people. Because you're crazy enough to walk barefoot along the edge of the sea when it's freezing cold. Because you tell very bad jokes at work. Because you use a pink penlight at work and you actually thought about covering it in glitter. Because you make fabulous sandcastles. Because,' he said finally, 'I love you. Heart, body and soul. I love you. Marry me, Lisa.'

She was silent for so long he knew she was going to say no.

'I'm sorry. My mistake.' He got to his feet. 'I'd better leave.'

'No.' She grimaced. 'I don't mean, no, I won't marry you. I don't know. I just…' She spread her hands. 'I don't know what to say.'

'How you feel about me would be a good start,' he said wryly. Because he still didn't have the faintest idea.

'I've never been in love before. Never let a relationship get that serious. I mean, I've had boyfriends. But it was always kept light. For fun. I haven't wanted to spend for ever with any of them.'

Did that include him? Ice trickled down his spine. Please, please, let her feel differently about him.

'But you—you're in my head, all the time,' she whispered. 'I know when you walk into Resus, even if I'm busy and my back's to the door.'

That kind of awareness… He felt it, too. And it felt a lot like love to him.

'You make me feel as if I can do absolutely anything—drive on ice, do a tricky surgical procedure in difficult conditions, anything. But what if I lose you, Joel? What if I lose you, the way my mum lost my dad?'

Was that what was worrying her? That she'd turn into her mother? 'Then you'll find the strength to go on. For our children's sake. And you'll go on being that same brave, beautiful, capable woman you are now.'

'My mum told me not to be scared to love,' she said. There was a distinct wobble in her voice. 'She said it's worth it.'

'And she's right.' He reached down to take her hand, pulled her to her feet and held her close. 'Listen to us. I'm terrified I'm going to be a failure as a husband—again—and I'll lose you and our baby. You're terrified to let me close in case you lose me. So why don't we let all the fears go and try dealing with them together?'

She was trembling in his arms. But she was also, he noted, holding him back. Her palms were splayed against his back and her cheek was resting against his chest.

'It's going to be fine,' he said softly. 'We're going to make it, Lisa. We just have to give each other a chance. I love you. If you love me too, we'll be just fine. Sure, we'll make mistakes along the way, but we'll make them together. And we'll fix them together, too.'

'I do love you. And I want to be with you. But…' Her voice was thick with tears.

'But?' he prompted gently.

'But I can't say yes to marrying you. Not until we've talked it over with Beth. It's not fair to her. We need to give her time to adjust. She might not even want me in her life.'

Oh, he was pretty sure his daughter felt the same way as he did. Wanted Lisa to be part of their family. But he also knew Lisa wouldn't take his word for it—that she needed to her it from Beth herself. He dropped a kiss on her hair. 'So if it's all right with my daughter, you'll marry me?'

'I…' She swallowed. 'Yes.'

'Then let's go ask her.'

'What, now?'

Her voice sounded very slightly quavery. He pulled back slightly so he could see her eyes. 'Lisa Richardson, have you just turned chicken on me?'

'Yes,' she admitted.

He smiled. 'I really don't think you need to

worry, honey. But I need to pick her up from Hannah's. Why don't you come with me?'

'And ask her?'

'Not necessarily.' He shrugged. 'Just say hello. See where it goes from there. And if it feels right…ask her.'

Sitting in Joel's car was…weird. The only time they'd been in a car together before, Lisa had been driving and Joel had been in hell. This time he was driving. It didn't help that she hated being a passenger. And right now she was going round in circles in her head.

Marriage. Babies. A family. Everything she'd always planned to avoid. Everything she'd thought she didn't want. Lisa Richardson, future emergency department consultant, trauma specialist and mainstay of the helicopter rescue team: that was how she'd always seen herself.

'Do I have to give it up?'

'What?' Joel sounded completely lost. Duh. Well, of course he couldn't read her mind.

'Air rescue.'

'While you're pregnant, yes. It'll be too much of a risk for you and for the baby.'

Hmm. He'd put her first, not the baby, she noticed.

'But when you've recovered from the birth, you'll do what feels right for you,' he continued. 'If you want to be a stay-at-home mum or go back to the ward part time or even stay as a full-time doctor, that's fine by me. I'm not giving up the coastguard and I don't expect you to give up the air ambulance.' He flashed her a smile. 'It's called teamwork. We'll sort it out between us, find what's right for us as a family. And I happen to know a very, very good childminder who'll back us up if we're both on the same shout.'

'You've got it all planned out, haven't you?'

'Not quite. It all pretty much hinges on you saying a certain little word to a certain question I asked you.'

Yes. Yes, I'll marry you.

But could she do this? Could she step into a ready-made family? Could she take that risk of loving Joel and Beth and their baby?

Right now her brain felt too fried to take it all in.

He didn't push her to talk to him, just switched the radio on and tuned it to a classical station. Soft, relaxing music filled the car and she was half dozing by the time he parked outside Hannah's.

'Um—had I better stay here?' she asked.

'Up to you.' He brushed her cheek with the backs of his fingers. 'I'm not ashamed of you. And Hannah's not a gossip. But if you feel more comfortable waiting here, that's fine.'

'I...'

He grinned. 'Stay put. I'll be back in a couple of minutes.'

True to his word, he wasn't long. She could see Beth holding his hand and chattering non-stop and skipping down the path. And then the little girl paused, pointing to the car.

Lisa knew exactly what she was asking.

She also knew the second that Joel answered, because Beth actually ran to the car and tugged at the doorhandle.

'Lisa, Lisa!' She threw her arms round her. 'I haven't seen you for ages and ages and ages, and I asked Daddy if you could have a sleepover with us, and he said no.'

Sleepover? Lisa gave Joel a speaking look. He'd need to explain that later.

'Did you help Daddy in the rescue?'

'No, I was still driving back from London. I just…bumped into your dad and thought I'd come and say hello to you.'

Beth beamed at her. 'You really came just to see me?'

'Yep.'

'Oh!' She bounced with delight, and started chattering about school and the story they'd had and the pictures they'd drawn and how she'd played weddings with her best friend Emma.

At the word 'wedding', Lisa glanced at Joel. He mouthed, 'I'll sound her out.'

He crouched down beside his daughter. 'How would you feel about me getting married again, kitten?' he asked.

'Married? You mean, I'd have a new mummy?' Beth asked.

'Um, yes,' he said.

She frowned. 'Would she be nice, like Lisa?'

Joel glanced at Lisa, 'I told you so' written all over his expression.

'How about if it *was* Lisa?' he asked, keeping his voice steady and neutral.

Beth's mouth opened wide, and then she smiled. 'Oh, yes!' She turned to Lisa. 'Will you marry my daddy? And can I be your bridesmaid?'

Again, Lisa glanced at Joel.

'Your call,' he mouthed.

He'd already asked her to marry him—because he wanted her for himself. He'd even put it in writing. And now Beth was making the same request. The little girl wanted Lisa to marry her father. Wanted her to be part of their family.

She smiled. 'I think that's a yes. To both.'

Beth whooped and hugged her. 'So we'll be a proper family, like everyone else in my class.'

'Yes,' Joel said. His eyes, as he looked at Lisa, were pure gold.

'Oh.'

Joel clearly picked up on his daughter's tone, because he asked, 'What's the matter, kitten?'

'Josh in my class, he's going to have a baby sister 'cos his mummy got married last year. Do you always have babies when you get married?'

'Not always. But sometimes, yes,' Joel said.

Lisa tensed. Was this where it was all going to go wrong? Would Beth feel threatened by the idea of a new baby? Would she think that meant they didn't want her any more?

'I think I'd like a baby sister,' Beth said solemnly. 'We could call her Isobel. That's a really pretty name.'

Joel smiled. 'We'll see what we can do. I can't guarantee it, though. You might end up with a baby brother.'

Beth thought about it. 'That's OK. I don't mind having a baby brother.' But then her smile dimmed. 'My mummy was going to have a baby. She died. You're not going to die if you have a baby, are you?' she asked Lisa.

'No, honey, I'm not.' Lisa sat down again and scooped her onto her lap. 'Lots of your friends have got mummies, yes?'

'Ye-es.' Beth's lower lip wobbled, and Lisa stroked her hair.

'And lots of your friends have got little brothers or sisters, right?'

Beth nodded. 'And big ones.'

'They were all babies once, inside their

mummies' tummies,' Joel said, as if he could read Lisa's mind.

She gave him a grateful smile, glad he was on her wavelength.

'And their mummies are still around, aren't they?' he asked.

Beth looked as if she was concentrating. 'Yes,' she said finally.

'So when I have your baby brother or sister, I'm still going to be around,' Lisa reassured her. 'Though I'm going to need your help.'

'My help?' Beth seemed surprised.

'Oh, yes. Big sisters have really important things to do.' Lisa kissed the tip of Beth's nose. 'Like teaching the baby songs.'

'I'm good at songs,' Beth said thoughtfully. 'And stories. I can do a really squeaky voice for the "Three Little Pigs". Daddy does a really good Big Bad Wolf.'

'That,' Lisa said, smiling at both Beth and Joel, 'sounds perfect.'

Everything was going to be fine.

EPILOGUE

Nine months later

JOEL found himself singing along to the radio on the way home. Ha. If someone had told him a year ago that he'd be this happy, he'd have considered having them sectioned.

Then, his life had been lonely, full of guilt, knowing that he'd been trying his best for his daughter and falling way short of the mark.

Now, he was married to the woman he loved and he had two beautiful daughters: the family he'd always wanted. Beth adored Lisa; on their wedding day, just after they'd walked down the aisle, Beth had asked Lisa if she could call her 'Mummy' now she was married to them both. Lisa had crouched down to hug the little girl, heedless of her dress, and had said in a choked whisper, 'I'd love that. I'd be so *proud* to be your mummy.'

Even the memory brought a lump in his throat. But it was a lump of happiness, not choking misery. The same lump he felt when he remembered Isabella's entrance into the world, saw the love and joy on Lisa's face echoing his own feelings.

Lisa had made everything all right in his world. She'd even charmed his parents; she tried hard to make them feel as included as they wanted to be in his family. Made sure they had all the grandparent paraphernalia of photographs of the children and footprints from Isabella and drawings from Beth, but without the noise and mess they couldn't cope with.

And, even more amazingly, he'd made things right in her world. Made her part of a family again. Taught her not to be scared of loving someone.

When he pulled up outside their house, he noticed that Lisa's car wasn't there. It was the school holidays, so he knew she wasn't on the school run or taking Beth to ballet lessons; she'd probably gone over to see her mother. Ella had moved up from London, and Beth had taken a shine to her new grandmother—one who was quite happy to get down on the floor with her and play princesses and ponies. The kind of grandmother he knew Beth had always wanted but which his own mother wasn't able to be, the sort who read stories and had a dressing-up box and played games and didn't get annoyed about mess or noise.

He'd give Ella a ring and maybe walk up there and take them all out for dinner. They might have an extra reason for celebrating tonight, though he needed to talk to his wife about it first.

He was halfway through making himself a cup of coffee when the outside of the fridge caught his eye.

Magnetic letters. There were always magnetic lower-case letters scattered over the outside of the fridge. Usually spelling 'beth' or 'isabella' or 'lisa', or 'i love daddy'—or whatever tricky words were on Beth's spelling list from school that week.

They'd been rearranged into a message.

gone 2 beach
join us when u get home

Joel smiled. He really should have guessed that was where they'd be. Even though it was March, and it wasn't exactly warm, the beach was Lisa's favourite place. And she was firmly backed up in that by his daughter. Even if the waves were fierce and the wind was howling, they loved the sea.

He skipped the coffee and drove down to the harbour. At least at this time of year it was easy to find a parking space.

And his heart contracted sharply when he rounded the corner and saw them.

His family.

Isabella was in her rocker seat, clearly well wrapped up and asleep, and Lisa, Beth and Lisa's mother were engaged in making an enormous sandcastle. Monty, Ella's black Labrador, was stretched out next to Isabella's seat, clearly having appointed himself as guard dog. None of them noticed him until he was near enough to call out—and then Lisa waved and Beth ran to him.

'Daddy! We've been waiting for you to come and you've been *ages*,' she said, hugging him.

'Come and see our sandcastle.' She slid her hand into his and pulled, skipping on the sand beside him until they reached the sandcastle.

He said hello to Ella, and then kissed his wife. Slowly. Lord, he loved her. Loved her warmth, her scent, her taste. *Loved* her.

'Daddy, does snogging make you have babies?' Beth asked.

Snogging? Since when had his daughter known that word? Joel broke the kiss and choked with laughter. 'No.'

'Good. Because Josh at school snogged Emily and you shouldn't have babies unless you're married,' Beth said, looking very serious.

Joel had to bite his lips hard to contain his smile. 'Uh-huh,' he said carefully.

'Why don't you two go for a walk on your own?' Ella suggested.

'Why, Nana?' Beth asked.

'Something to do with someone growing out of their bike, maybe.' Ella tapped the side of her nose. 'And we have a sandcastle to make.'

More like so he could kiss his wife stupid without an audience. Joel mouthed, 'Thanks,' over the top of Beth's head. He drew Lisa to her feet and shepherded her round the cliffs.

'Your mother's a wise woman.' He brushed his mouth against hers. 'I've been thinking about kissing you for the last half an hour.'

'Only half an hour?' she teased.

'It was a concentrated half an hour.' He slid his hands over her buttocks and drew her closer.

'Oh-h-h.'

He was gratified by the way her eyes widened, and she blushed.

'And later,' he said, 'I'll show you just how concentrated.'

'Oh, good.'

He loved that little hint of wickedness in her voice. 'But this is a public beach and our family's making a sandcastle not very far away.'

'Yeah. Our family.' She kissed him lightly. 'We've been lucky.'

'And we're going to stay that way.' He stole a kiss. 'Got some news for you.'

'What sort of news?'

'The consultant's post.' He stole another kiss. 'It's mine if I want it.'

'Oh, Joel!' She hugged him. 'That's marvellous news. Congratulations.'

'I haven't said yes yet.'

She frowned. 'Why not?'

'It means more responsibility. Meetings. And it might take up more time.' He stroked her face. 'I promised you I'd never put my job before my family.' Been there, done that, knew better now.

'Of course you won't. Because you're learning to delegate. And if you ever do start forgetting us, Beth and Isabella and I will paint pink glittery messages all over your most important reports.' She reached up to kiss him. 'Joel, it's what you wanted. Emergency department consultant. You'll be brilliant. Go for it.'

Encouraging him. Just as she'd encouraged him to apply for the post in the first place.

'Then I think,' Joel said, 'I might be taking us all out to dinner tonight. To celebrate my promotion.'

She smiled. 'I have some news for you, too: I had my six-week check-up today with the GP.'

The light in her eyes told him exactly what the answer was, but he asked anyway. 'And?'

'And,' she said, 'everything is more than fine. So I think we'll have a private celebration, later.'

Joel kissed her lingeringly, until they were both out of breath. 'That,' he told her, 'is on account.'

'Tease,' she pouted.

'Mmm.' He stole one last kiss. 'Come on. Let's go tell our family.'

Arms round each other, they walked back towards Ella, the children and Monty.

And Joel knew with a certainty that everything was going to be just fine.

MEDICAL™

—∿— *Large Print* —∿—

Titles for the next six months…

November

A BRIDE FOR GLENMORE	Sarah Morgan
A MARRIAGE MEANT TO BE	Josie Metcalfe
DR CONSTANTINE'S BRIDE	Jennifer Taylor
HIS RUNAWAY NURSE	Meredith Webber
THE RESCUE DOCTOR'S BABY MIRACLE	Dianne Drake
EMERGENCY AT RIVERSIDE HOSPITAL	Joanna Neil

December

SINGLE FATHER, WIFE NEEDED	Sarah Morgan
THE ITALIAN DOCTOR'S PERFECT FAMILY	Alison Roberts
A BABY OF THEIR OWN	Gill Sanderson
THE SURGEON AND THE SINGLE MUM	Lucy Clark
HIS VERY SPECIAL NURSE	Margaret McDonagh
THE SURGEON'S LONGED-FOR BRIDE	Emily Forbes

January

SINGLE DAD, OUTBACK WIFE	Amy Andrews
A WEDDING IN THE VILLAGE	Abigail Gordon
IN HIS ANGEL'S ARMS	Lynne Marshall
THE FRENCH DOCTOR'S MIDWIFE BRIDE	Fiona Lowe
A FATHER FOR HER SON	Rebecca Lang
THE SURGEON'S MARRIAGE PROPOSAL	Molly Evans

⊚™ MILLS & BOON®
Pure reading pleasure

1007 LP 2P P1 Medical

MEDICAL™

Large Print

February

THE ITALIAN GP'S BRIDE	Kate Hardy
THE CONSULTANT'S ITALIAN KNIGHT	Maggie Kingsley
HER MAN OF HONOUR	Melanie Milburne
ONE SPECIAL NIGHT...	Margaret McDonagh
THE DOCTOR'S PREGNANCY SECRET	Leah Martyn
BRIDE FOR A SINGLE DAD	Laura Iding

March

THE SINGLE DAD'S MARRIAGE WISH	Carol Marinelli
THE PLAYBOY DOCTOR'S PROPOSAL	Alison Roberts
THE CONSULTANT'S SURPRISE CHILD	Joanna Neil
DR FERRERO'S BABY SECRET	Jennifer Taylor
THEIR VERY SPECIAL CHILD	Dianne Drake
THE SURGEON'S RUNAWAY BRIDE	Olivia Gates

April

THE ITALIAN COUNT'S BABY	Amy Andrews
THE NURSE HE'S BEEN WAITING FOR	Meredith Webber
HIS LONG-AWAITED BRIDE	Jessica Matthews
A WOMAN TO BELONG TO	Fiona Lowe
WEDDING AT PELICAN BEACH	Emily Forbes
DR CAMPBELL'S SECRET SON	Anne Fraser

MILLS & BOON®
Pure reading pleasure